'I want you, and you want me. It's mutual. So there's a pretty logical conclusion here.'

He traced her lower lip with his thumb, and Sara's lips automatically parted. 'Oh, good. I'm so glad you agree with me,' he said softly, and bent his head to kiss her. His mouth brushed against hers, the contact light and teasing and tempting her to respond. When she tipped her head back slightly, he deepened the kiss, offering and demanding at the same time.

Sara had kissed men before. Been to bed with men before. But this… This was something else…

TO TAME A PLAYBOY
Hot, sexy, and double the pleasure!
Modern Heat™ introduces
Kate Hardy's new playboy duet

PLAYBOY BOSS, PREGNANCY OF PASSION

BY
KATE HARDY

MILLS & BOON

MODERN *Heat*™

First published in Great Britain 2009
Harlequin Mills & Boon Limited,
Eton House, 18-24 Paradise Road, Richmond, Surrey TW9 1SR

© Kate Hardy 2009

ISBN: 978 0 263 87240 8

Set in Times Roman 10¼ on 11¼ pt
171-0509-53140

Printed and bound in Spain
by Litografia Rosés, S.A., Barcelona

Kate Hardy lives on the outskirts of Norwich with her husband, two small children, a dog—and too many books to count! She wrote her first book at age six, when her parents gave her a typewriter for her birthday. She had the first of a series of sexy romances published at twenty-five, and swapped a job in marketing communications for freelance health journalism when her son was born, so she could spend more time with him. She's wanted to write for Harlequin Mills & Boon since she was twelve—and when she was pregnant with her daughter, her husband pointed out that writing Medical™ Romances would be the perfect way to combine her interest in health issues with her love of good stories. Now Kate has also ventured into Modern Heat™ Romance too, and SURRENDER TO THE PLAYBOY SHEIKH is her ninth novel for this series.

Kate is always delighted to hear from readers—do drop in to her website at www.katehardy.com

Also by this author:

SURRENDER TO THE PLAYBOY SHEIKH*
HOTLY BEDDED, CONVENIENTLY WEDDED
SOLD TO THE HIGHEST BIDDER
ONE NIGHT, ONE BABY
BREAKFAST AT GIOVANNI'S

*To Tame a Playboy duet

Kate Hardy's Medical™ Romance duet—
The London Victoria:

THE CHILDREN'S DOCTOR'S SPECIAL PROPOSAL
THE GREEK DOCTOR'S NEW-YEAR BABY

For Michelle Styles—
good friend and fellow history aficionado—with love

PROLOGUE

'So what's her name, Luke?' Karim asked as he and Luke left the squash court.

'Whose?'

'The woman who's distracting you.' Karim gave his best friend an appraising look. 'Why else would I beat you by this much of a margin?'

Luke smiled despite himself, recognising his own question thrown back at him. The difference was, when *he'd* asked, there had been a woman distracting Karim—the woman who was now his wife. It wasn't the same for Luke, who had no intention of letting anyone that close to him. 'Not my social life. Work,' he said economically.

'Sounds as if you need some TLC, Lily-style. Come back with me and have dinner with us.'

'What, tonight? It's hardly fair, dumping a guest on Lily at the last minute.'

'You're not a guest.' Before Luke had the chance to protest further, Karim had already speed-dialled home. Two minutes later, he hung up and, in his best attempt at Luke's East London drawl instead of his own cut-glass accent, said, 'Sorted.'

Luke, knowing that Karim was laughing with him rather than at him, gave in gracefully. It wasn't as if he was going to find a replacement for Di tonight. The temp agency was sending someone first thing in the morning, and hopefully the temp

would stay long enough for him to find proper maternity cover
for his personal assistant.

Even though that was going to take time he'd prefer to use
more profitably, he was just going to have to be patient.

Ha. Patient. A word that barely existed in his vocabulary.
When Luke wanted something, he went for it. He didn't waste
time. And having to wait around on other people's schedules
was the quickest way to drive him crazy.

To his relief, Karim didn't press him to talk on the way back
to his home. Karim simply let them in, headed straight for the
kitchen and kissed his wife lingeringly.

'Put the girl down. For pity's sake, you've been married for
three months. You should be over this stage by now,' Luke said
from the doorway.

Lily just laughed. 'You really *are* out of sorts, Luke. Here.
These will keep you going until dinner.' She gestured to a plate
of canapés on the island unit.

Luke suddenly realised that he'd forgotten to eat lunch—
he'd been too busy fixing things to think about food, and now
he was ravenous. He needed no second invitation to grab a bar
stool and work his way through the canapés. 'Thanks, Lily.'

As always, her food was wonderful. Restorative. 'Fabulous,'
he said after the first mouthful.

She inclined her head in thanks. 'So are you going to tell us
what's bugging you?' she asked.

He sighed. 'I just wish I understood why on earth women
want babies in the first place. Di hasn't stopped throwing up
since the day she did the pregnancy test, and—' He stopped
abruptly as he caught the glance that Karim and Lily were
sharing. The kind of glance that could mean only one thing.

He grimaced. 'Sorry. I don't have a shred of manners. I
apologise—and of course what I just said doesn't apply to you.
I'm really pleased for you both.'

'You'd better be,' Karim said, 'as you're going to be an
honorary uncle.'

For all Luke knew, he might already be an uncle.

He blocked the thought. The decision he'd made was harsh, but it was also the only one he could have made. If he'd stayed, he would've gone under and ended up like the rest of the men in his family.

Doing time.

'Thank you,' he said politely. 'I'm very honoured. When's the baby due?'

'Six months.' Lily laughed. 'You're really trying hard to say the right thing, aren't you, honey?' She ruffled his hair on her way to the fridge.

She was treating Luke as if he were her big brother and it made him feel odd. As if there were an empty space deep inside him. A space where he really wanted to be part of a big family.

Which was ridiculous. He was perfectly fine on his own. Much, much better than he had been as part of a family. Been there, done that, no intention of taking a backward step. 'I'm only being nice because you're cooking and I want to be fed,' he retorted.

She laughed even more. 'Don't give me that. I know you're just a pussycat.'

Karim was laughing, too; he'd scooped his wife onto his lap and he had both hands resting protectively round her abdomen.

Luke joined in the fun. 'For you, Lily, I could be.' Then he grinned. 'But unfortunately you have a husband who might not be too happy about that, so I'll settle for being fed.'

'Your wish is my command,' Lily teased back. 'So what's wrong? Your secretary's got morning sickness?'

'And lunchtime sickness. And afternoon sickness. My office is a mess, she hasn't been there to do a proper handover to the temps—when they turn up, that is—and neither have I, and…' He broke off and shook his head in exasperation. 'I've had enough of the chaos. I've sent Di home for the rest of her pregnancy.'

Lily looked worried. 'Luke, I don't mean to interfere, but…is that legal?'

Luke knew exactly what she wasn't asking. 'Don't worry, Lily,' he said dryly. 'She's on full pay and her job's open until she decides what she wants to do. But right now she's not capable of doing her job properly and it's unfair to expect her to keep up with me when she's feeling so rough. And I need someone who can sort this mess out before I lose any more opportunities.'

'Someone who's a good organiser.' Lily looked thoughtful. 'I might just be able to help you out there. My favourite supplier, Louisa—her sister's a freelance office troubleshooter.'

'A what?' Luke asked.

'Organised, efficient, and good at sorting things out. You know those reality TV programmes about people who come to your house and make you sort out your clutter? Well, that's apparently what Sara does in real life. Except in an office. And she does the sorting out for you.'

If the woman was no good, Lily wouldn't have mentioned her. Luke knew that Lily realised the importance of business networking—that your recommendations reflected on you. And this sounded like the solution he needed. 'Do you have her number?'

'No, but I've got her sister's, which is the next best thing.' Lily disappeared for a couple of minutes, then returned with a card. 'Here.'

Luke read the card. 'Fleet Organics.'

'They do apple juice, apple balsamic vinegar and—well, everything else you'd expect from an organic orchard,' Lily explained. 'Ask for Louisa, tell her I gave you the number and say that you need to talk to Sara.'

'Thanks.' He slid the card into his wallet. 'And if this troubleshooting woman's that good…'

'She might be busy,' Lily warned.

'Hmm, that's what someone told Karim about you. But he still charmed you into cooking for him,' Luke reminded her with a grin. 'I'll call her. See what she can do for me. Thanks for the tip.'

Lily checked something in the oven. 'OK, it's done. Go through to the dining room, you two.'

Karim and Luke did her bidding.

Luke took a first mouthful of the food. 'Lily, this is wonderful. If you ever decide you're bored with being a princess, you can come and be my housekeeper.'

'She won't be bored,' Karim informed him. 'Find your own princess.'

'I'm not a prince,' Luke countered. 'And I don't need a princess.' What he wanted was a good assistant at work, a part-time housekeeper who would sort things while he was out and wouldn't nag him about being a slob, and a string of girlfriends who wanted to have fun and accepted the fact that he wasn't looking for anything permanent.

Apart from the assistant problem—which, hopefully, this office troubleshooter would help him fix—that was exactly how his life was, at that moment.

And it suited him just fine.

CHAPTER ONE

SARA checked the address in her diary. Yes, this was the place. A former warehouse converted to a mixed-use residential, office and retail block, all sparkling clean brick and lots of glass. The ground floor was full of bijou shops and coffee bars—she made a mental note to check them out later, and drop in some of the family business cards—and she guessed that the top two floors were offices. It looked as if the architect had taken advantage of a partially collapsed roof at one end and had put up a tower with one wall of sheer glass—though it had been sympathetically done and looked in keeping with the building. That, she guessed, was the residential part of the building; the rooms on the side with the glass wall would have stunning views of the Thames.

You'd need a small fortune to be able to afford that sort of flat. But, hey, she was fine with the room she'd begged in her oldest brother's flat. Just because she didn't have a place of her own, it didn't mean she was a failure. She had a family who loved her as much as she loved them, a great social life and a job she enjoyed. She didn't need anything else.

She took the stairs to the first floor, where a receptionist sat behind a light wood desk.

'Can I help you?'

'I have an appointment to see Luke Holloway. Sara Fleet,' she said.

'Through the corridor, last door on the right,' the receptionist said with a smile.

Luke Holloway. He'd sounded crisp on the phone, the kind
of man who knew what he wanted and didn't waste time. Which
made it all the more surprising that he needed an office troubleshooter. She usually dealt with people who stuffed things into
drawers and scribbled things on sticky notes which they promptly
lost and didn't have a clue what a filing system or diary was—
and Luke hadn't given her that impression when he'd asked her
to meet him at his office. So what kind of man was he?

Well, she was about to find out for herself.

The last door on the right was closed. She knocked and waited.

'Come in.' The voice sounded slightly harassed.

She'd been expecting someone in a sharp suit and handmade
shoes; the man leaning back in a chair, talking on the phone
with his feet on the desk, looked more like a rock star. He was
wearing a black round-necked sweater that she guessed was
cashmere, teamed with black trousers, and his short dark hair
was expensively tousled—the kind of haircut that made him
look as if he'd just got out of bed. Teamed with eyes the colour
of cornflowers and the most sensual mouth she'd ever seen, it
was enough to make Sara's libido sit up and beg.

Though she knew better than to mix business and pleasure.
This man was her client. Well, *potential* client. They'd agreed
to meet today and discuss the situation; she'd learned in the past
that someone might sound reasonable enough on the phone, but
in person they were a nightmare to work with, so it was easier
to discuss things face to face. Particularly as she prided herself
on her ability to judge people quickly yet fairly: in business,
she'd never once been wrong.

Personally… Well, now wasn't the time to start brooding
over that.

He put his hand over the receiver. 'Are you Sara?' he
asked quietly.

She nodded.

'Good. I'm Luke. Sorry about this. I'll be with you in two minutes—take a seat or a look round the office, whichever you prefer.'

And he was as good as his word; he'd wrapped up the call before she'd had time to absorb more than the fact there were two desks in the room, both with state-of-the-art computers and completely clear work surfaces, and a bank of filing cabinets. The view from the office window over the river was stunning; she could see ships sailing down the Thames, and on a sunny day like this the water sparkled.

'Right—I'm all yours,' he said.

The thoughts that put in her head… Very, very unprofessional thoughts. Thoughts of him lying naked on crisp cotton sheets that were just about to get seriously rumpled.

Sara pushed the idea away and really hoped that her face hadn't turned as red and hot as it felt. What the hell was wrong with her? She never, but never, started fantasising about her clients. Even the good-looking ones.

Though Luke Holloway was a little more than good-looking. He was the most gorgeous man she'd ever seen. The sort whose smile would make any woman's heart feel as if it had just done a somersault.

'Can I get you a coffee?' he asked.

'Thanks. That'd be nice.' Though what she really needed was a cold shower.

'Bathroom's over there, if you need it.' Luke indicated the door in the far corner.

Oh, no. Please don't let her have said that thing about cold showers out loud. Then her common sense kicked in. Obviously he meant if she needed the loo. 'Thanks, I'm fine.'

He opened another door to a small galley kitchen. 'Milk, sugar?'

'Just milk, please.'

He added milk to one cup and sugar to another, then took a tin from the cupboard and removed the lid. 'Help yourself.'

Extremely posh chocolate biscuits.

Clearly her amusement must have shown on her face because he laughed. 'My only vice. Well, almost.'

She caught the gleam in his eyes and could guess the other one. It dovetailed with the thoughts she'd had when he'd told her he was all hers. And it made her mouth go suddenly dry. She had to make a real effort to force her mind back to business. He wanted a troubleshooter, not a lover.

She wasn't in the market for a lover in any case. She liked her life as it was. Happy and *single*. Uncomplicated.

'So what makes you think I can help you?' she asked.

'You come highly recommended,' he said simply.

'So,' she countered, 'do you.'

He inclined his head, acknowledging the compliment. 'Lily warned me that you might be busy.'

'Usually, I am.' She shrugged. 'I'd planned to take the summer off to do a bit of travelling. Spend a month in Italy or Greece.'

'Good food, decent weather and plenty of sandy beaches?'

'Plenty of ruins,' she corrected. A beach holiday, sitting still and doing nothing, was her idea of boredom. She liked exploring. 'It's one of the perks of being self-employed—I can choose when I want to take a holiday.'

He handed her a mug of coffee, then picked up his own mug and the tin of biscuits and ushered her back into the office. 'Most self-employed people have to be forced to take time off.'

Was he talking about himself? She looked straight at him. 'It's important to take time off. If you don't refill the well, you end up with burnout and you're no good to anyone. Good time management helps a lot.'

He didn't look convinced, but at least he didn't try to argue with me. Which was good. After Hugh, Sara had had enough of workaholic men. Ha. After Hugh, Sara had had enough of men, full stop. She kept her relationships light, flirty—and absolutely not committed.

'My office isn't usually this disorganised,' he said, shepherding her back into the main room and indicating a chair.

'Disorganised?' The place was spotless. Unless she was missing something huge.

'As I said on the phone, my personal assistant's pregnant and she's been off sick a lot. I've had temps in, but Di—that's my assistant—hasn't been able to brief them properly, and I haven't been here enough to do it myself.' He rolled his eyes. 'Today's temp didn't even bother turning up. I was talking to the agency when you came in, asking them what had happened.'

Sara couldn't resist the impulse to tease him. 'Are you telling me you're so scary that the temps have got your name on a blacklist and refuse to come and work for you?'

'I'm not scary in the slightest. I just expect a fair day's work for a fair day's pay. And if you can't do basic things like answering the phone politely and taking a proper message, then you shouldn't take a job as a PA.' He raked a hand through his hair. 'Actually, one of the temps was excellent, but when I asked if I could have her back for a long-term assignment, the agency said she'd already been given a placing somewhere else and wasn't available.' He propped his elbows on the desk and rested his chin on his hands. 'Which leaves me in a mess. I need someone to go through all the filing and put my office back into the order I'm used to, and to keep this office ticking over until Di decides whether she wants to come back after she's had the baby.'

'I can do the first bit,' Sara said, 'but I do short-term assignments only. Maternity cover—that's way too long a time for me.'

'Understood.'

'So how much filing are we talking about? Because, unless I'm going mad, I can't see any filing at all.'

Luke walked over to the other desk and removed a large cardboard box from underneath it. It was full of papers, stuffed in haphazardly. 'This,' he said. 'I know, I know. Do the filing daily and it's a small job. Leave it, and the next thing you know it's overwhelming. But Di felt too rough to do it. She knows I hate clutter, so she put it all into this box out of the way, meaning to do it later.'

'Except now she's not here, and your temps have consistently ignored it.'

'Exactly. And Di usually weeds the files. My guess is she hasn't done that for a while, either.'

'So would I get carte blanche to reorganise your filing system?'

'If it's a genuine time-saver, yes; if you're trying to justify your bill, no.'

She liked the fact that Luke Holloway was this blunt. It meant she'd know exactly where she stood with him. No pussyfooting around, no hiding behind a façade of being a polite, bumbling upper-class Englishman, the way that Hugh had.

Not that Luke could pretend to be upper-class. Not with that accent.

'So what exactly is it you do?' she asked.

'Are you telling me you didn't look me up on the Internet?'

She flushed. Of course she had. 'It didn't tell me very much. You're twenty-eight and a self-made millionaire.' And his girlfriends were all the model type—tall, long legs, exotic looks and impossibly shiny dark hair. He dated a lot, was on the guest list at the best parties and changed his girlfriend frequently. Extremely frequently. 'But newspaper stories and online gossip columns aren't always accurate.'

'It didn't tell me much about you, either. Apart from the fact that you don't have your own website.'

So he'd looked her up, too?

Well, of course he had. Even if she'd come recommended. Luke was the kind of man who'd pay attention to detail. 'I don't need a website. My clients come from word of mouth.'

'Which is the best form of advertising. It's accurate and it can't be bought.'

How come they were discussing her business? She was meant to be finding out about his. 'You still haven't answered my question,' she pointed out.

'I buy and sell businesses.'

She blinked. 'You're an asset stripper?' No way was she going to work for someone like that. Even if he did come highly recommended, and had the sexiest mouth she'd ever seen. She had standards. Standards that, post-Hugh, she wasn't going to compromise.

'No. I get bored easily and I like a challenge.' He shrugged. 'So I buy failing businesses and turn them into going concerns. And, once they're back on their feet, I normally manage to arrange a management buyout.'

So the people who put the work in with him to sort out the company reaped the rewards. A man with a conscience, then.

The complete opposite of Hugh.

Not that she was going to think about Hugh the Betrayer.

'I'm good at solving problems.' He rolled his eyes. 'Usually. This is the exception that proves the rule.'

'What sort of businesses?'

'Sport and leisure. Gyms, health clubs, spas…and I'm thinking about expanding a bit.'

'And you do all this on your own?'

'With a good PA. And decent managers in each business who are savvy enough to talk to me well before something becomes a major problem—and who come to me with solutions rather than expecting me to sort it all out.'

Luke liked the way Sara Fleet questioned him. The way she cut right to the nub of the problem. He could work with her.

'So why are you freelance?' he asked.

'I guess it's the same thing as you—I'm good at solving problems and I get bored easily.'

Better and better. He could *definitely* work with her.

'And I like decluttering and sorting out mess.'

'Are you mad?' He slapped a hand against his head. 'Sorry. That wasn't meant to be an insult. I loathe filing, so I'm grateful to find someone who actually likes it. I don't understand you at all but, believe me, I'm grateful.'

'I like putting things into order. I suppose I'm a bit of a neat freak.' She glanced round his minimalist office. 'Looks as if you are, too.'

'Look, I'm being rude here, but your sister tells me you had a first-class degree. How come you're working as an office troubleshooter?'

'A glorified filing clerk, you mean?'

He blinked. Had he been that obvious, or had she just heard the question too many times? 'I wasn't going to be quite that blunt, but yes.'

'It's information retrieval. I suppose I could've been a librarian or archivist,' she mused, 'but I like the challenge of sorting out new places. My family nag me about my degree, but frankly I'd had enough of academia and all the backbiting and I couldn't face staying on to do my doctorate. So I temped for a bit, while I decided what I really wanted to do with my life.' She shrugged. 'Then Lou worked out that what I love doing most is a business asset, and I'd be better off working for myself than working for an agency.'

He ignored the mention of her family. It was irrelevant to his business. He didn't care if she could trace her family back ten generations and was best friends with all her fourth cousins three times removed. If she could do the job, that was all that mattered. And so far she seemed pretty clued-up. 'It sounds sensible to me.' He paused. 'So do you do other things, besides decluttering?'

'Such as?'

The first thing that came into Luke's head shocked him. He'd only just met the girl, for pity's sake. Sara was the complete opposite of his normal type—well, apart from the fact that she had long legs. Her straight blonde hair was pinned into a neat chignon, whereas his girlfriends always had dark hair with that just-got-out-of-bed look, and her eyes were sharp and blue instead of a wide, soulful brown. She was dressed totally for business, in a little black suit teamed with a demure cream-coloured top; a choker of black pearls added a classy note.

But then there were the shoes.

Killer heels. Shiny. And bright pink.

A touch of the exotic.

He took a deep breath, willing his libido to go back to sleep. This wasn't appropriate. Even if Sara Fleet did have a gorgeous mouth and legs he'd like to see more of. This was *business*. And he wasn't going to act on the impulse to ask her out to dinner. Or the even stronger impulse to yank her into his arms, unpin her hair and kiss her stupid.

Focus, he warned himself.

'I don't know how long it's going to take you to sort this lot out. Or how long it's going to take me to find maternity cover.' He gave her a speculative look. 'I think your mind works the same way that mine does. You're going to get bored sorting out my filing.'

'Your information retrieval system.'

He laughed. 'Don't try to dress it up in fancy words. It's a box of filing, and you know it.'

'Plus a potential overhaul of your systems, if you show me what you already have in place. What else did you have in mind?'

Again, he thought of her body wrapped round his. Which was crazy. Apart from the fact that Sara Fleet wasn't his type, he knew better than to mix business with pleasure. It always ended in tears.

Except for Karim and Lily. But again they were the exception that proved the rule.

And he knew he was going out on a limb here, but his hunches were usually right. 'The kind of business I'm looking at—I could do with a female viewpoint. An honest one.'

She frowned. 'What sort of business?'

'A new venture, for me.'

'Which tells me *so* much.'

He loved her sarcastic tone. It meant she'd speak her mind,

rather than telling him what she thought he wanted to hear. And he valued honesty and straightforwardness. 'I'm looking at buying a hotel. I have three or four options, and I want to check them out, so it means there'll be some travelling involved. Would that be a problem?'

'No. Justin won't mind.'

Justin? Obviously her partner, he thought. Good. That made her very firmly off-limits. Because he only dated women who were single and who didn't have wedding bells in their eyes. Sara was already spoken for, so he could lock away that instant attraction and simply work with her. 'Fine. Right—systems.' He took a swig of coffee, then talked her through the bank of filing cabinets, answering her questions as they went along. 'That's the paper side of things. Computer…' He drew a chair round to his side of the desk, then tapped into the computer and flicked through the various programs. 'Accounts, payroll, correspondence, past projects, current projects. All bog-standard stuff. I assume you can deal with spreadsheets and graphs.'

'Yes.' She asked a few more questions—sensible ones, and not just for the sake of it, he noticed—and then it was decision time.

He knew what he wanted. So he did what he always did and played it straight. 'So that's the set-up here.' He paused. 'Would you be prepared to sort out my office and act as my PA until I find maternity cover?'

'Yes.' She told him her hourly rate.

'That's less than the agency charges,' he remarked.

'Because agencies,' she said dryly, 'pay temps about half the rate that they bill the clients. To cover overheads and profit.'

'True.' And he liked the fact she was sharp enough to realise that. 'Though you could get away with charging more than you do.'

'I thought clients were supposed to haggle for a reduction in fees, not an increase?'

He spread his hands. 'A fair day's work deserves a fair day's pay. If you're as good as I hear you are, you'll be worth it.'

She inclined her head in acknowledgement of the compliment. 'When do you want me to start?'

He glanced at his watch. 'How about…now?'

CHAPTER TWO

LUKE was surprised at how quickly Sara settled in. By the beginning of the following week, it felt as if she'd always worked with him. He'd persuaded her to man the office and take phone messages while he was out, and Sara turned out to be brilliantly organised. If he was out of the office she emailed the messages to him so he could act on them if they were urgent. Or she dealt with queries herself and sent him an email to tell him what she'd done.

He loved the fact that she used her initiative instead of running to him with questions.

And whenever Luke reached a point in his work when he was about to stop and make himself a mug of coffee, Sara was there before him. Just as he was about to look over to her desk and ask if she wanted a coffee, too, she'd place a mug on the coaster on his desk. Rich, smooth coffee, the exact strength he liked, with no milk and one spoonful of sugar. Perfect.

'Have you been talking to Di or something?' he asked when he'd finished his coffee.

'How do you mean?'

'Because you second-guess me, the way she did. It's almost like having her back—and she had four years to get used to the way I work.'

Sara laughed. 'No, I haven't talked to her. Not about *you*, at any rate. She called the other day to see how everything was and I told her to put her feet up with a mug of ginger tea and stop feeling guilty.'

'Good. That's what I told her, last time she rang.' He paused. 'So how did you…?'

'Know how you work? Observation,' she said. 'Most people have routines.'

'So you're saying I'm set in my ways?'

She spread her hands. 'Work it out for yourself, boss,' she teased.

'You're just as set in your ways,' he retorted, slightly nettled.

'Meaning?'

If she was going to be straight with him, then he'd be straight with her. 'You're here on the dot of nine, you always take exactly an hour's lunch break and you leave at the dot of five. And you never, ever work late.'

'Because I'm good at time management.' She returned to her own desk. 'Besides, the longer the hours you work, the more your productivity drops. By the third day of working late, you're actually running behind.'

'How do you work that out?'

'Easy.' She scribbled something on a piece of scrap paper, then walked over to his desk and put it in front of him. 'One curve. The x axis is time, the y axis is your productivity rate. Now, would you agree that it's higher in the morning, when you're fresh, and lower at the end of the day, when you're tired?'

'Yes.' Though he could see exactly where this was heading, and he had a nasty feeling that she'd boxed him neatly into a corner.

'So if you're not fresh, because you're tired from the previous day, you'll start further along the x axis, from a lower productivity point, as if you've already worked a couple of hours. And the more days you work late, the further along the x axis you start each morning.' She folded her arms. 'My point, I think.'

'Hmm. And what about personal variables? Some people are best first thing in the morning, others are better later in the day.'

'True.'

'And some people thrive on working long hours. Point to me.'

'Some people *think* they thrive on it,' she countered. 'I hate that culture where you have to be seen to be in early and work late. Presenteeism isn't good for you. The way I see it, if you want to get more done, you need to work smarter, not harder.' She frowned. 'Do you ever take time to smell the roses, Luke?'

'I don't need to smell any roses.'

She looked at him over the edge of her rimless glasses—glasses, he'd noticed, she only used for computer work. 'Yes, you do. Everyone needs to refresh themselves, or they'd burn out. So what do you do?'

He shrugged. 'I go to the gym.'

'You own several gyms. So that doesn't count. It's work.'

'No, it's not.'

'Can you tell me, hand on heart, that whenever you go for a workout or what have you, you don't start appraising the place and thinking about how to maximise the use of the gym?'

'When I play squash or have a workout, I focus on what I'm doing. Otherwise,' he said with a grin, 'I'd be at the bottom of the squash ladder.'

'Whereas you're at the top?'

He spread his hands. 'Top or second. Whatever.'

'And the moment your workout or your match ends, you switch over to business, don't you?'

'It's who I am.'

'No,' she said. 'It's what you do. Who you are is…' Her voice faded and for a second he caught an odd look in her eyes. Something that made his pulse skip a beat. But then it was gone, and he had to remind himself she was off-limits.

'So aren't these parties you go to any fun?'

'They're overrated,' he admitted. 'Or maybe I'm getting old. But, yeah, I'm starting to find them boring.'

'Is that why you change your girlfriend so frequently, too?'

'Probably.'

'Maybe,' she said thoughtfully, 'you're seeing the wrong kind of woman.'

He nearly asked what kind of woman she thought fitted the bill. But maybe it was better not to know. Better not to wonder if a certain bossy blonde would fill the empty spaces he almost never admitted were in his life.

Before he realised what he was doing, he asked, 'How about you?'

'I go to the theatre and the cinema with my friends. We might go out for a meal—anything from a pizza to tapas to Thai, as long as it's good food. Or I'll go home to be spoiled by my parents and play with my toddler niece and take the dogs for a long run in the orchard.'

Hmm. She hadn't mentioned her partner. Or maybe the guy was so much part of the furniture that she didn't bother mentioning him by name.

But there was a bigger danger area here. Even if she had been free, she was clearly very close to her family—a world away from his own life. So it was definitely better to keep things strictly business with her.

'So I take it you don't work weekends?' he asked.

'Absolutely not.'

'That's a pity,' he said. 'Because I could do with you this weekend.'

'How do you mean?'

'I'm going to see a hotel,' he explained. 'And, as I think you have a gut feel for what needs fixing, I'd be interested to see what you thought of it.' He spread his hands. 'Of course I'd pay you for your time, because it'd mean an overnight stay, but if you came with me I'd respect your right to clock-watch—and I promise you can stop answering my phone and let it go to voice mail at five o'clock on the dot. And you can take a couple of days off next week—paid—to make up for the time.'

She gave him a speaking look at the phrase 'clock-watch', but when she spoke her tone was mild. 'This weekend.'

'Unless your partner will have a problem with it?'

'Partner?' She looked mystified.

'Justin,' he enunciated. Saying the man's name helped him remember that she was spoken for. That she was off-limits.

Her face cleared. 'Oh, *Justin*. He isn't my partner. He's my oldest brother. I share a flat with him.'

Luke's heart missed a beat. He'd managed to keep his hands off Sara so far by telling himself that she was attached and therefore off-limits.

Now it turned out that might not be the case.

Given how blank she'd looked when he'd asked her about her partner…it made him pretty sure that she wasn't attached at all.

All of a sudden the room seemed to shrink. Right now, Sara was close enough to touch.

And, oh, he wanted to touch.

Taking her to Scarborough would be a spectacularly bad idea. Way too full of temptation—temptation he wasn't sure he'd be able to resist.

Then he realised that she was speaking. 'Sorry?'

She rolled her eyes. 'Pay attention.'

'Yes, ma'am. Would you mind repeating that?'

'Please,' she prompted.

He'd like to hear her saying that word in other circumstances. In a different tone. All husky and sensual and on the edge of losing her control.

All the blood in his body went south, and he had to swallow hard and close his eyes for a moment to regain control. He just hoped she didn't look down at his lap, because the evidence of his thoughts was pretty clear. 'Please.'

'I said, did you mean telling you honestly what I think?'

'Given that half my clients will be female, I need a female point of view. Which, obviously, I don't have. And you tell it like it is—which is what I want to hear. You don't have a hidden agenda.'

'You said the weekend,' she said. 'Would you want to leave on Friday?'

'Yes. We'll stay Friday evening and Saturday, and come back Sunday. And I'll let you have Monday and Tuesday off to make up for the time, as well as paying you while we're away.'

'It's not about the money.'

He raised an eyebrow. 'It should be. You're running a business, not a charity.'

'Staying in a hotel with you.' Her eyes narrowed. 'That means separate rooms, yes?'

'Of course it means separate rooms. I'm asking you to join me as my consultant. My colleague.' Even though he would've liked to ask her for a different reason, he knew that mixing business and pleasure was a stupid idea. Besides, although it had turned out that Justin was her brother, not her partner, she hadn't actually *said* she was unattached. 'So your partner won't mind?'

'I already told you, Justin's my brother.'

'Which is why,' he pointed out, 'I didn't ask you again if Justin would mind. I asked you if your *partner* would mind.'

'I'm single, if that's what you mean.' She lifted her chin. 'I could ask you the same. Will your partner mind me accompanying you?'

'I'm not seeing anyone right now,' he said, 'so it's not a relevant question. That's why I asked you to come with me: to give me a female viewpoint.'

'What about your mother? Your sister?'

'I don't have either.'

She flushed. 'I'm sorry, Luke. I didn't mean to stamp on a sore spot.'

'You weren't to know,' he said lightly. He knew Sara would assume that his mother was dead; he had no idea whether his mother was still alive or not, but he'd lost her a long time ago. Even before he'd walked out on his family, nearly half a lifetime before. 'Let's change the subject, hmm?'

'Good idea.' She looked relieved. 'Um…what sort of dress code are we talking about?'

He shrugged. 'Whatever you want. I should warn you now,

t's not a posh hotel. It might've been, once. But now it's…'
He stopped, trying to think of a nice way to put it.

'Shabby genteel?' she suggested.

'Pretty much.'

'And you're going to turn it around. Restore it to its
former glory.'

'If all the figures stack up and my gut feeling tells me to go
for it—yes, that's the idea.' And he needed to get out of here.
Before he did something utterly stupid. Like swivelling his
chair round, taking Sara's hands and pulling her off balance so
she landed in his lap and he could kiss her until they were both
dizzy. He glanced at his watch. 'Right. I have a meeting. I'd
better go.'

'There isn't a meeting in your diary.'

Well, of course she'd know his schedule. She was acting as
his PA. 'I forgot to put it in,' he fibbed. 'I'm going to see the
temp agency. Interview a few potentials.' And that was exactly
what he was going to do. Even though they weren't expecting
him. Because right now he needed to put space between himself
and Sara. For both their sakes.

Sara forced herself to concentrate on the task in hand when
Luke had gone. Strange how the office felt empty without him.

And she still felt guilty. Not about the banter—she was
pretty sure he enjoyed it just as much as she did, and she knew
that he'd come up with a dozen valid reasons why working
overtime was good for you, to counter her arguments—but
about the fact she'd inadvertently hurt him. There had definitely
been a flash of pain in his eyes when she'd mentioned his
mother and he'd told her he didn't have one. It was a fair bet
that the rest of the men in his family were the sort who'd bury
themselves in work rather than discuss their feelings, and Luke
himself had admitted that he dated a different girl every couple
of weeks. So he probably didn't allow himself to get close to
anyone in case he lost her, the way he'd lost his mother.

A man alone.

It made her want to put her arms round him, give him a hug and tell him that everything would be fine.

Not that she had any intention of doing that. Because she knew it wouldn't stop at a hug. Several times in the last week she'd looked up and met Luke's gaze; he'd quickly masked his expression, but not before she'd been aware of the flare of heat. Desire. Interest.

Exactly the same way she felt. And, the more time she spent with him, the stronger those feelings became.

Perhaps she should've refused to go to Scarborough. They'd be stuck in a car together for a long journey. They'd spend the whole weekend in each other's company. And, even though it was business, it would be all too easy for it to slide into something else.

Uh. *Slide*. Bad analogy. Because now she had other pictures in her head. X-rated ones.

She dragged in a breath. 'Don't be so stupid. You've already been there, done that and got your heart broken,' she told herself loudly. 'Remember Hugh? He was just as much of a workaholic as Luke is. It didn't work then and it won't work now.'

Though Hugh's mouth hadn't had such a sensual curve as Luke's.

And whereas she'd eventually been able to wipe Hugh's kisses from her memory, she had a feeling that she wouldn't be able to do the same with Luke's. She'd get hurt. Badly.

She'd just better hope that he managed to find a PA to cover for Di, and she could finish this job before the temptation got too much for her.

CHAPTER THREE

SARA had managed to compose herself by the time Luke returned—literally five minutes before she was about to leave. 'Any luck?' she asked.

'No. Clearly it's not my week for finding new staff. So if I can ask you to stay just a little longer?'

'Yes,' she said, before her common sense had a chance to stop her.

'Good.' He sat on the edge of his desk. 'Sara, I bulldozed you a bit about Scarborough.'

'A bit?' She arched an eyebrow.

'OK, a lot,' he admitted. 'And I know it isn't fair, giving you such short notice to rearrange your weekend. So don't feel you have to do it.'

'It's all right. I wasn't doing anything in particular,' she said. 'I had vague plans to go to the cinema with friends, but nothing definite.' Nothing that couldn't be changed. 'Besides, it'd be nice to get out of London and go to the seaside.'

'We're going to Scarborough to *work*,' he reminded her.

She smiled. 'Maximum eight hours a day. Which means we'll have time to smell the roses—well, the sea air, anyway.'

He didn't take the bait. 'As long as you're sure it's not a problem.'

'It's not. But I do insist on having a paddle in the sea. And one of those whippy ice creams with a chocolate flake stuck in it.'

He shrugged. 'Do what you like in your lunch break.'

'So you're too chicken to paddle?' she teased.

'Too *busy*,' he retorted.

'A five-minute paddle isn't going to take much out of your day. And the break will do you good.'

'Refilling the well?' There was a slight edge to his voice.

'Good. The man's learning,' she said, resisting the urge to walk over to him and ruffle his hair. Touching would be a bad idea. She might not be able to stop at ruffling his hair. And she needed to be professional with him. She wasn't looking for a relationship right now; even if she had been, Luke wasn't the man for her. He kept too many barriers round himself. She wanted someone less complicated. 'Right. I emailed your messages to you as they came in, there's a report on your desk next to a pile of letters that need signing—and I'll see you tomorrow.'

'OK. And, Sara?'

She paused by the door.

'Thanks. I do appreciate you. Even if I don't say it.'

'You know, that's why you're on the temps' blacklist,' she said with a grin. 'You're too grumpy, too uptight, and you grunt instead of talking.'

'There isn't a temps' blacklist—and I don't grunt.'

'No?' she teased.

'No. Go *home*,' he said, flapping a hand at her and going back to the proper side of his desk.

No doubt he was going to work late again tonight, Sara thought. From what she'd seen of Luke, she was beginning to wonder where on earth the press got those photographs of him at parties and why his name was linked with a string of women. As far as she could see, he didn't have a social life. He just worked.

Maybe on the way to Scarborough she could start to draw him out a bit. Make him talk to her. Find out what made him tick.

* * *

n the Tuesday, to Sara's surprise, Luke was actually in the
ffice at lunchtime. 'I'm going to call down to the sandwich
ar and order something. Do you want anything?'

This was where she knew she ought to smile politely and
y thanks for the offer, but she'd get something while she
ent out for her usual lunchtime walk.

Though she couldn't resist the mad impulse to try to reform
m. To teach Luke Holloway to smell the roses. To make the
mile on his mouth reach his eyes. 'Thanks, that'd be lovely.
ut I've got a better idea. Instead of having sandwiches deliv-
ed here, why don't we pick up some lunch on the way?'

'The way where?' he asked.

'Call it an experiment in boosting productivity. If you go for
walk at lunchtime, you get more done in the afternoon. It's
omething to do with getting extra oxygen to your brain.'

'This,' he said, 'sounds to me like one of your flaky ideas.'

'I'm not flaky. I'm *enlightened*,' she said loftily. 'And you're
workaholic.'

He held both hands up in the classic surrender pose.
iuilty as charged, m'lud.' Except his grin was completely
irepentant.

'Seriously, Luke, taking a complete break and doing a bit of
.ercise is good for you.'

'Exercise.'

How did he *do* that? How did he manage to make her think
' sex, whatever he said? She wasn't sure if it was the glint in
s eyes, or the fact that when he spoke she couldn't take her
es off his mouth. 'Walking,' she said, then immediately took
swig of water from the glass on her desk, hoping he'd think
r voice was husky simply because she needed a drink. And
e really, really hoped her thoughts hadn't shown on her face.

He glanced out of the window. 'You have a point. It's a nice
y. A walk would be good.'

She checked her watch. 'Let's leave in half an hour.'

He raised an eyebrow. 'What happened to working smarter?'

'Just trust me,' she said. If they went now, the place she ha[d]
in mind would be crammed with office workers. If they took [a]
late lunch, it would be just how she liked it. How she wante[d]
to share it with him.

'You're the boss. We'll order the sandwiches anyway, [to]
make sure they don't run out. I recommend the crayfish wra[p.]
Unless you're allergic?'

'No, that'll be fine. I'd love to try the crayfish.'

Half an hour later, after they'd picked up their lunch, sh[e]
ushered him towards the tube station.

'I thought you said we were going for a walk?'

'We are. Not here.'

'We're going to the Tower of London?' he asked whe[n]
they left the train at Tower Gateway and headed toward[s]
Tower Hill.

'Not quite. Trust me,' she said, leading him down a narro[w]
path and surreptitiously glancing at his face to see his reactic[on]
when they arrived at their destination.

'A church?' Covered in ivy.

'Not quite.' And then she led him inside, gratified by the utt[er]
surprise on his face, followed quickly by an expression of di[s]
belief and…was that delight?

'Wow. I had no idea this place was here.'

'St Dunstan in the East. It was bombed in the Blitz, but instea[d]
of knocking it down the authorities turned it into a garden.'

Instead of pews there were park benches, instead of a fo[nt]
there was a fountain, and instead of glass fronds climbir[g]
shrubs filled the arched window frames.

'Refilling the well,' she said softly, sitting on one of th[e]
empty benches and patting the seat next to her. 'If I'm workir[g]
in the city, this is where I come for lunch. Outside the lunc[h]
rush hour, that is.'

'It's beautiful,' he said. 'And so quiet. You'd never believ[e]
you were in the middle of the city.'

'Exactly. It reminds me a bit of home,' she said.

'You miss the country?'

She nodded. 'But I love the buzz of the city, too. So I suppose have the best of both worlds—I live here in London, but I can o home to Kent whenever I want.'

'The garden of England.'

'Absolutely. We're spoiled with castles and stately homes nd gardens on our doorstep.'

'I've always lived in London,' he said reflectively.

'So you've never spent any time in the country?'

'The occasional weekend. Nothing much.'

She smiled at him. 'You'll have to come back with me some me. I'll show you some of my favourite places.'

'Are you asking me on a date, Sara?'

For a second, she couldn't breathe. The air felt as if it were rackling with electricity—even though the sky was a clear blue nd there wasn't so much as a single wispy white cloud, let lone purple-grey storm clouds.

A date.

She'd meant it as a throwaway but genuine offer. To share some f her favourite places and spread a little sunshine into his life.

But it could be construed a different way. That she'd just sked him out.

Her heart skipped a beat.

Would he accept?

Another missed beat.

Did she *want* him to accept?

The world suddenly felt precarious, and she backtracked. 'ast. 'Not a *date* date. An offer to a friend—because I like you, nd I think we could be friends.'

'What, even though you boss me about?'

She was relieved that he'd slipped back into teasing banter. 'hat, she could cope with. 'Hey, I'll have to be bossy if I'm avigating.'

'What about sat nav?' he countered.

'You can't beat local knowledge.'

'True. Point to you.' He regarded her seriously. 'The way yo
see life…everyone's a potential friend until proven otherwise
aren't they?'

She thought about it. 'I suppose so,' she admitted. It was th
way she'd been brought up—around people who loved her an
always showed their affection.

'Don't you get disappointed?' he asked.

'Not often.' She had with Hugh, but he was the exceptio
that proved the rule. 'Are you saying that you see everyone a
a potential enemy, then?'

'Hardly. I'm not the paranoid type.'

'But you don't let people close.'

He shrugged. 'It makes life much less complicated.'

It also made life lonely, she thought. Not that there was an
point in saying so. She had a feeling that Luke would claim h
didn't need anyone and that his life was just fine as it was. 'Yo
see the glass as half empty, then?'

He smiled, but it didn't reach his eyes. 'It's obvious you se
it as half full. I'd say it's simply half a glass. Telling it as it i:
no flowery description.'

His words were light, but she could hear the warning signa
she might want to be friends, but he'd keep her at a distance
She kept the conversation completely impersonal for the re:
of their lunch break, telling him what she knew about th
history of the church, and he seemed to relax again with he
And, although Luke spent most of the afternoon either on th
phone or in meetings, he was back at his desk just before sh
left the office for the evening.

'Sara?'

'Uh-huh?' She glanced up from her computer and wa
rewarded with a smile that did actually reach his eyes. A smil
that did seriously odd things to her insides.

'I just wanted to say thanks. For sharing that garden wit
me today.'

'Pleasure.' And it warmed her that he'd enjoyed it. 'See you tomorrow.'

'Yeah. Have a nice evening.'

'You, too.' On the surface, it was polite office chit-chat. Though Luke wasn't the sort to do chit-chat. He was always charming, but she knew he hated wasting a single second. So the fact he'd bothered to thank her and wish her a nice evening… Maybe he was learning to trust her. Opening up to her just that little bit.

Though Sara was completely thrown the next morning, when she walked in to find a beautiful bouquet of roses on her desk, all pink and cream. 'What's this?'

'You made me stop and smell the roses yesterday. I thought I'd do the same for you today,' he said. His smile was just the wrong side of wicked. 'A thanks for helping me out.'

She shrugged. 'Strictly speaking, you're my client. You're paying me to help you out.'

'If you had the builders in, you'd make them tea and bring them cake and make a fuss of them so they did a good job for you, yes?'

'Ye-es.' Where was he going with this?

'Same thing,' he said. 'Except you're not a builder. You're a girl.'

'You noticed?' she deadpanned.

'I noticed.'

There was a flare of heat in his expression that triggered a corresponding flare in her body. To the point where she really needed a cold shower. She took refuge in being sassy. 'Basically, this is a business expense.'

'No. It's from me to you, to say I appreciate you.'

'And so you should.' No way was she going to let him know that his comment, even more than the flowers, had just turned her into mush. She buried her nose among the blooms. Their scent was sweet, yet heady. 'Thank you. They're beautiful. How did you know I'd like pink roses?'

He coughed and gestured to her shoes.

She smiled. 'Busted. OK, so it's my favourite colour.' She breathed in their scent again. 'Thank you, Luke. These really are lovely.'

And when she made them both a coffee and put a mug on his desk, she gave in to the impulse and kissed his cheek.

'What was that for?' he asked.

'Just to say I appreciate the roses.'

'Pleasure.' But he was staring at her mouth.

Just as she was staring at his.

Wondering.

She was used to giving hugs and kissing cheeks and ruffling hair. It was how she'd grown up, in the middle of a close and noisy and affectionate family. But kissing Luke's cheek just now, being close enough to smell his clean scent and feel the softness of his skin against her lips…that hadn't been her best idea. Because it had made her all too aware of him: an awareness that could be dangerous.

An awareness that grew and grew over the morning. Luke had a lunchtime meeting—one that had been in his diary since before she'd started working with him, so she knew it wasn't an excuse to avoid her. She had lunch on her own, sitting on a bench overlooking the river. Giving her time to think.

Things were definitely starting to change between her and Luke; although Sara still didn't really know what made him tick, she liked the glimpses he'd allowed her to see so far. Liked them enough to want to know more. To get to know him properly. And…

She took a sip of her ice-cold water. If she let her thoughts go much further in that direction, she'd need to up-end the bottle over her head to cool her down.

* * *

'I'm pulling rank,' Luke said the next day. 'We're having a working lunch.'

She coughed. 'Lunch is meant to be a *break*.'

'Refilling the well. Yeah, yeah, you told me.' He flapped a dismissive hand. 'But I need to brief you a little bit about this weekend.'

'The operative word being "little". I thought you wanted me to do it completely as a mystery shopping kind of thing?'

'Even mystery shoppers need a brief. Look, it's time for lunch. If you don't have anything better planned, there's a very good pizza place round the corner.'

He'd dressed it up as a business thing—but he knew full well that wasn't what he was offering. This was the same as her offer to him the previous day of a weekend in the country: a date that wasn't a date.

He'd enjoyed spending time with her in that tiny, perfect garden. And even though the alarm bells were ringing in his head, warning him that this was a dangerous game, he wanted more. Something about this woman made him want to break the rules. Get to know her better.

'Sounds good to me. As long as we split the bill.'

'You,' he said, 'are the boss.'

She laughed. 'Yeah, right.'

He loved the way she laughed. It made him feel as if the sun had just come out after a dull, grey morning.

And why a beautiful, clever, warm woman with a sense of fun was still single was beyond him. He wouldn't have been surprised to learn that Sara Fleet had been snapped up the second she'd turned sixteen.

Or maybe that was it. Maybe she was a widow. True, she was very young to be a widow—but life wasn't always fair, and if she'd loved her husband that much... Then again, she was using her maiden name.

And why was he speculating about something that was

none of his business? He shook himself. 'Let's go so we can beat the rush.'

They arrived in time to grab a seat under one of the umbrellas on the terrace overlooking the river.

'Do you recommend anything?' Sara asked.

'It's all good. The pizzas are wood-fired, so they're fabulous. Wine?'

'Thanks, but I'll stick to sparkling water. If I drink at lunchtime, it makes me want to curl up and go to sleep.'

Luke suppressed the thought that he'd like to watch her curled up and sleeping, satiated after making love. He was meant to be keeping this strictly business. But there was something about her that drew him.

They settled on pizza, and sharing focaccia bread and a simple salad. But when the waiter arrived, he was clearly struggling to write down their order.

'Luke, would you mind if I ordered?' Sara cut in gently.

He spread his hands. 'Be my guest.'

She said a few words in what Luke guessed was Italian, and the waiter beamed at her before bursting into an absolute torrent of language. Sara was smiling back, speaking just as rapidly. Luke didn't have a clue what they were talking about, but he liked the lilting sound of the words from her mouth.

The waiter was clearly also charmed, because he disappeared into the kitchen and returned almost immediately with a rose in a vase.

A pink rose.

She thanked him, and he gave her a deep bow before disappearing to see to another customer.

Luke grinned. 'Trust you to make sure we take time to smell the roses.'

She flushed. 'Sorry. I wasn't showing off, just then— Gianfranco was struggling and it's hard enough dealing with customers without the language barrier. He's only been in

England for a week; he's come over to work in his uncle's business in his gap year.'

Luke was impressed that she'd found out so much information in such a short space of time. Then again, there was something about Sara that made you want to trust her.

Which made her dangerous.

He pushed the thought away. 'It was kind of you to help out. So you speak Italian fluently.' Then he remembered. 'And I've stolen your week in Italy.'

She shrugged. 'I hadn't booked my ticket, so it wasn't a problem. I can go to Sorrento some other time.'

'Well, I feel guilty.'

'Good.' She grinned at him. 'You can buy me pudding to make up for it.'

That zest for life, that love of food…and it was so refreshing, after the time he'd spent with women who nibbled on a lettuce leaf and made a fuss about counting carbs. 'Deal. So do you speak any other languages?'

'French. A bit of German. And I can scrape by in Greek, provided I have a dictionary.'

'Impressive.' He smiled ruefully. 'I never really learned languages at school. I haven't needed to, for work.'

'You can speak the universal language, though. Money.'

'Well enough.' He shrugged. 'Have you been to Scarborough before?'

'No—we always tended to go south, down to the coast at Sussex. You?'

'A long time ago,' he said. It was one of the few memories from his childhood that was happy.

'You're right. The pizza's excellent,' she said after her first mouthful. 'And so's the bread—I love it that they do it with rosemary here. It reminds me of Florence.'

'So you like ruins?' He remembered her degree was in history, so it was pretty obvious she'd be interested in that kind of thing.

'It's the way the past still echoes down through to the present, and the beauty never fades.'

When she talked about something she enjoyed, she was really animated, he noticed. And her enthusiasm was infectious. 'You could've been a teacher. You would've really inspired your classes,' he said.

She wrinkled her nose. 'I did think about it. But there's so much red tape in education—it would just suck the joy out of it, for me. Besides, I like what I do now.'

And if she'd been a teacher, she wouldn't have walked into his life.

Although Luke didn't join her in having a pudding, he indulged in a rich, dark coffee, and when they returned to the office he was shocked to discover they'd been out for an hour and a half. Considering that lunch for him was usually just long enough to eat a sandwich... He made a mental note to put in the extra time that evening, and forced himself to concentrate on figures and phone calls for the rest of the afternoon.

He'd just replaced the receiver when she put a mug of coffee on his desk. 'Problem?'

'Nothing major. The guy I was playing in a league match tonight—he needs to reschedule because something important cropped up at work. Which means I have a court booked but no partner.' He looked speculatively at her. 'I don't suppose you...?'

'Absolutely not.'

'I thought you said exercise was good for you?'

She shook her head, laughing. 'I'm hopeless at racquet sports. Justin tried to teach me, and I was so embarrassingly bad that he had to admit defeat.'

'I could teach you.'

Her eyes met his and awareness zinged through him. Both knew he hadn't been talking about just squash.

'Thanks for the offer, but it's not really me.' This time, she was the one to give the speculative look. 'Though if you're at a loose end...'

'What?'

'You didn't look that convinced at lunchtime when I told you why I loved ruins. Come and see something with me. And you don't have an excuse—you just told me your squash match was cancelled.'

'Has anyone told you that you're a bulldozer in disguise?'

She laughed. 'Yup. So are you game?'

He should say no. Use the time to work. But his mouth didn't seem to be working in synch with his brain. 'Sure.'

'Something' turned out to be the British Museum. 'I love the courtyard here,' she said. 'It's the light and shade—just lovely.'

A big, wide open space with a glass ceiling, triangles radiating out from a central column. He could see exactly what she meant.

He'd never really spent any time in museums. But when she took him to see the Egyptian mummies and the Roman mosaics, he could see it through her eyes and was enchanted.

'Haven't you ever done this before?' she asked, clearly surprised.

'I guess when you live in a place, you take it for granted and don't get round to doing the touristy things.'

'True, and doing them on your own's not such fun because you don't get to share them and talk about them with someone.' She reached out and took his hand for a moment, squeezing it. 'Maybe we can come back together some time.'

'That'd be nice.'

What really shocked him was that he meant it. He wanted to spend time with her. He liked the sound of her voice and could've listened to her all day when she told him about the things that clearly grabbed her attention. And he *really* liked the touch of her skin against his.

Ah, hell. This wasn't supposed to happen. He didn't *do* relationships. He always had brief and mutually satisfying affairs with women who knew the score. Women who moved in the same glittering social circles. Women who didn't have wedding bells in their eyes or want him to meet their families.

Sara Fleet was a mass of contradictions. Efficient and businesslike, and yet warm and touchy-feely at the same time. He still hadn't quite recovered from that kiss on the cheek earlier that afternoon. God only knew how he'd stopped himself turning his face to hers and capturing her mouth.

And right now her hand was curled round his.

It was oh, so tempting. All he had to do was raise her hand to his lips. Kiss the backs of her fingers. Turn her wrist over and press his mouth to the pulse point, see if it jumped as hard and fast as his own heart was beating right then.

It didn't matter that they were standing in the middle of a public place. The rest of the world just faded away. He could pull her into his arms. Cup her face. Lower his mouth to hers. Taste the sweetness on offer…

'Luke?'

Uh. He really was losing the plot. He never, but never, allowed himself to be distracted like this. 'Yeah, fine,' he said, not really sure what he was agreeing to, but the warmth of her smile promised him it was something good. 'Listen, I'd better let you go. You'll need to pack for tomorrow.'

'And you, no doubt, are planning to squeeze in some work.'

'A teensy bit.' Which might just stop him thinking about kissing her.

'You,' she said, 'are impossible.'

'So I've been told.' He disentangled his fingers from hers and was dismayed to find that he actually missed their warmth and pressure.

Not good at all.

He was twenty-eight, not thirteen. Time he remembered that and acted like it. 'Come on. I'll put you in a taxi.'

'I'm perfectly capable of getting the Tube.'

'I know. But humour me.'

'Depends.'

'On what?'

'I'll take a taxi,' she said, 'if you agree to paddle in the sea with me on Saturday.'

'And you say *I'm* impossible?' He rolled his eyes. 'Come on.' He hailed a taxi, paid the driver and waved her goodbye.

And the worst thing was, he couldn't wait to see her tomorrow.

'You,' he told himself loudly, 'need your head examined. She's a complication you don't need.'

Though he had a nasty feeling that he was protesting just a little too much.

CHAPTER FOUR

'IT'LL take us five hours to get there,' Luke said when Sara walked into the office the next morning. 'So we'll leave at two, when you're back from lunch. That way we'll get there at seven, we'll have time to unpack and have a quick shower and then we'll have dinner.'

Sara looked surprised. 'We're not stopping on the way?'

'Not unless you need a comfort break.'

'What about you?'

He wrinkled his nose dismissively. 'I'd rather just get there.'

'You're the boss.'

There was definite sass in her tone, but Luke didn't rise to the bait. He spent the morning in meetings and his lunchtime reading reports. Sara was back at two o'clock precisely, as he'd expected.

'Only one suitcase—and a small one at that?' he queried.

'We're only away for two days. Why would I need more?' She rolled her eyes. 'Clearly you mix with the wrong sort of woman.'

'Meaning?'

'High maintenance—the sort who can't open a door without checking for damage to their nails. And whose top drawer is full of make-up and emergency hair spray, and who travel with six changes of clothes per day.'

He laughed. 'Point taken. But it's refreshing.' Like her shoes, though he refrained from commenting. Today's were suede, in a deep teal colour to match her camisole top.

Then he wished he hadn't thought about matching shoes. Because it made him wonder if her underwear matched, too. And what she'd look like in just teal-coloured lacy underwear and those shoes and the black pearl choker, with her hair loose instead of worn up, and...

'I'll carry that. You can lock up behind us,' he said gruffly.

'I can carry my own case.'

'As you say, I mix with the wrong sort of woman. I'll carry the cases. And my laptop.' He lobbed the bunch of keys at her; as he'd expected, she caught them automatically. She gave him a speaking look, but locked up and followed him down the stairs to his car.

'Nice,' she said, clearly appreciating the sleek lines of his car, then frowned as he opened the back door. 'Aren't you going to put the cases in the boot?'

'There's no room.'

'What, you're taking half a filing cabinet with you or something?'

'It's a hybrid car,' he said. 'The one downside is that the battery takes up most of the space in the boot.'

'You've got an eco car?' She raised an eyebrow. 'I'd have expected you to go for a really flash sports car. A limited-edition thing.'

He laughed. 'Absolutely. I have my name on the list for an eco sports car that's going to be on sale in about...oh, seven years' time. But this'll do for the time being.'

'It doesn't look like the one my sister drives. Hers is eco too, but it's...well...' She wrinkled her nose.

'Ugly?' he finished. 'I'm with you all the way. Just because a car's environmentally friendly, it doesn't have to *look* worthy. You can be green and still have fun.'

'But you don't have fun,' she pointed out.

'Oh, but I do,' he purred. He moistened his lower lip, aware that she was watching every move, and enjoyed the way her colour heightened. Good. So she wasn't quite as cool and collected as she made out.

He stowed their cases on the back seat, then opened the passenger door for her. 'And don't give me a hard time about being perfectly capable of opening a door yourself.'

'Would I?' She gave him a wicked grin, then sat on the seat and swung her legs gracefully into the car in a move that could've come straight from finishing school. And her knee-length skirt rose up just enough to make his own temperature rise accordingly.

Well, it served him right for playing games.

And he was going to need the air con on full to cool him down.

'This car was really expensive, wasn't it?' she asked when he slid into the driver's seat.

'That depends on your definition of expensive.' He gave a half shrug. 'I like to drive in comfort.'

'I can see that. A real wood and leather interior. Justin would just drool over this.' She laughed. 'Well, he'd drool more if it was an E-type Jag.'

'If it was a red one, so would I. But classic cars need a lot of maintenance and a lot of time.'

'Which you're not prepared to spend.'

He smiled ruefully. 'You said it.'

'Hmm. I really didn't have you pegged as an eco warrior.'

He indicated the building behind them. 'This place is carbon neutral. It's one of the reasons I chose the office space.' She didn't need to know that he owned a sizeable chunk of the building. 'And my hotel chain is going to be carbon neutral, too. Using as many local materials as possible.'

'That's why Dad turned the orchard organic when my grandad let him take over the reins,' Sara said. 'It means our costs are higher, but it's worth it.'

Something else they agreed on.

It was beginning to scare him, just how well she matched him.

He wasn't in the market for a relationship. Didn't want the commitment. Didn't need the hassle and misery he knew that a family could bring.

He really needed to get his head straight and concentrate on this new venture instead of thinking about how sexy the curve of Sara Fleet's mouth was.

'So why Scarborough?' Sara asked.

'I'm looking for a hotel in a spa town. Scarborough was famous for its waters in its heyday. I'm looking at another in Cromer, and one in Buxton.'

'Why not somewhere closer to London, so you don't have so much travelling time?'

Because Scarborough was the only place he could ever remember having a family holiday. Not in a hotel—they'd stayed in a little guest house—but they'd had a week of sun and sea when he was tiny. Before his mother had turned into a shadow of herself and his father had let them both down. Not that he was going to explain that to Sara. It was irrelevant. 'I'm just exploring my options at this stage,' he said.

'So this place in Scarborough…'

He shook his head. 'If I tell you the facts and figures it'll colour your view. I want to know what you think of the place as a customer. What's good, what's bad, what's missing.'

'Do they know you're thinking about buying it?'

'No. As far as they're concerned we're just customers, and that's the way I want it. I'm not trying to catch anyone out. I just want to see things as they are on a normal day—not when they've made a special effort.'

For the first three hours of the journey, they worked. Sara answered his phone, made appointments, sorted out his schedule for the next three weeks and talked business.

And then she stopped.

'Five on the dot?' he teased.

'Five on the dot,' she agreed—and, to his horror, switched his phone off.

'What are you doing?' he asked.

'I've put your phone on to voice mail. Turning it off means it'll be much less stressful for you than hearing the three rings before your voice mail cuts in—because, knowing you, you'll start nagging me to bend the rules and answer it. And no, you're not putting it onto hands-free and answering it yourself.'

Bossy didn't even begin to cover it. And Luke was too surprised to argue.

'Righty. Now this is a fabulous sound system.'

'It has nineteen speakers,' Luke said.

'Nineteen? That's excessive.' She groaned. 'Boys and their toys. Rupert—he's my baby brother—he would just *love* this. Let's see. What have we here?' She fiddled with the playlist. 'Oh, I should've guessed. Dinosaur rock.'

'It's not dinosaur, it's indie. And it's great to drive to,' he protested.

'Yeah, yeah.' Though at least she switched it on.

'I suppose you're into ballet music,' he retorted.

'What makes you say that?'

'You're all posh and pearls,' he said with a grin. 'See, I can do stereotypes, too.'

She paused. 'Actually, I do like ballet music. And, before you ask, yes, I did have ballet lessons when I was young.'

'And piano and horse-riding?'

'Don't be chippy.'

'I'm not. It's just…how the other half live.' He gave her a sidelong glance. 'I can just see you in a tutu.'

'You don't wear tutus for practice,' she said loftily. 'You wear leotards and footless tights.'

He could imagine her in a leotard, the material clinging to her body. And then wished he hadn't, when his body reacted predictably.

'Anyway, I stopped doing ballet when I was twelve.'

'Why?'

'To be any good, I would've had to spend hours a day practising,' she said. 'And I didn't want to be a dancer when I grew up, so it wasn't fair for me to take a place in the class if it meant that someone who really wanted to dance missed out. But I enjoyed it while I did it.'

Ballet. That certainly explained the grace with which she walked.

'What about you?' she asked.

'No, I never fancied being a Billy Elliot.' He pushed away the thought that, if he had, his family would've put a stop to it. Ballet didn't exactly go with their lifestyle.

To his relief, she let it go and seemed contented enough to look out of the window and listen to music—the same music she'd just decried, he noted with wry amusement. And it was fine until the traffic information report on the radio cut through the music, at about the same time as he noticed the queue of traffic on the motorway.

'Oh, great,' he said, switching off the engine as they came to a halt at the end of the queue. 'And we're miles away from the next junction, so I can't even take us cross-country to avoid the tailback.'

'Hey, it's not your fault. Accidents happen. We'll just have to wait for the road to clear.'

Though waiting wasn't one of his strong points. When he asked her for the third time to check the Internet on his phone to see if there was an update on the traffic situation, she sighed. 'You can't stand being still, can you?'

'No. I hate wasting time.'

'I doubt very much if anything's changed in the last five minutes. We're stuck,' she said dryly, 'so live with it.'

'Mmm.' He drummed his fingers on the steering wheel.

'You could always talk to me, to take your mind off it.'

Talk? In his experience, when women wanted to talk, it meant trouble. That they'd changed their minds about not wanting a commitment—and they expected him to change, too.

Then again, he wasn't in a relationship with Sara. Officially, they were working—even if she had clocked off. So that made things easy. 'Oh, you want a proper rundown on the hotel.'

She tapped her watch. 'Remember, it's gone five. I'm off duty. So no work talk.'

'What do you want to talk about, then?' He knew it was a mistake even as he uttered the words.

'You,' she said simply. 'I want to get to know you better.'

He wanted to get to know her better, too. Much more intimately. But he knew it was a bad idea. That it would turn his life upside down. And he'd fought too long and too hard to get where he was to throw it all away.

When he didn't reply, she sighed. 'OK. So you're the strong, silent type. Give me your hand.'

'Why?' But he did so.

She inspected his knuckles. 'Wow. No grazes. I'm impressed. What did you do, wear gloves?'

To stop his knuckles dragging on the floor, she meant. He couldn't help laughing. 'I'm not a Neanderthal, Sara.'

'You're not a new man either, I'd bet.'

'You want a *personal* conversation?'

She must've seen the warning glitter in his eyes because she flushed. 'Not that kind of personal. I just wondered what made you tick.'

'Same as most people. Oxygen and food.'

She rolled her eyes. 'You made your first million before you were twenty. Given that you're not a computer geek…at least, I don't think you are?'

She was fishing. Not good. He needed to head her off. 'No. I'm just good at economics.'

'So how did you find that out? You worked in a family business?'

His family had definitely had a business. Generation after generation had gone into it. But he'd chosen not to. 'No.'

'Then how?'

She clearly wasn't going to let this rest. And, given that all three lanes of the motorway were jammed solid, he couldn't go anywhere. So he'd tell her some of it. 'I was good at maths, and my teacher had a hunch.'

She didn't need to know it was the teacher who'd bailed him

out of the police station when his family had proved impossible to contact.

Ha. Everyone knew the rules: get caught, and you're on your own. It had been a waste of time even trying to get hold of his family, and the police had known it. They'd had to follow procedure—but they'd wasted little time before contacting his school.

And they'd struck gold.

So had he.

Literally.

'Hunch?' Sara queried.

'That I'd be good at economics as well as maths.' He smiled wryly. 'It didn't do much for my street cred, having extra lessons at lunchtime.' Not that anyone would've dared say anything to him about it. They knew who his family was. The school bullies chose targets without any implied muscle behind them.

'But it paid off.'

'Yep. I got a job on Saturdays and school holidays, working on a market stall.' Again, thanks to his teacher, who'd happened to live next door to the trader—and who'd guaranteed that Luke wasn't like his family and there wouldn't be any trouble. 'The original barrow boy, that's me.'

And he needed to get his patter back. Fast. Get her away from the subject of families. 'I talked the stallholder into giving me a share of the stall instead of an hourly wage, and put most of my profits back into the business. Worked out some new lines. And within a year we'd expanded. By the time I was fifteen, I had my own stall and I paid someone to work on it while I was at school.'

And he'd refused to launder any of the family's money. It had caused rows, but he'd stood his ground. And when his cousin had tried to teach him about family loyalty…that was where his other extra-curricular lessons had come in handy.

Boxing.

He'd broken his cousin's nose.

And it had sickened him, how easy it had been to fall into

the spiral of violence and crime. He didn't want to be like hi
family—and yet the only way to prove it to them had been t
act the way they did. Wrong, wrong, *wrong*.

Luke had also been the one to clean up his cousin's face and
take him to hospital. And when they'd returned to the house
he'd quietly explained to his family that he wanted to sta
straight. That he didn't want to have any part of what they did
And he'd given them an ultimatum: they had to accept that o
let him go.

They'd turned their backs on him.

Every single one of them.

Even his mother.

He'd learned then what family really meant. Toe the line o
you were out. Try to follow a different dream, and the
wouldn't be there to encourage you.

He was on his own.

So he'd packed and left that evening. Slept on the stree
because it was too late to find somewhere to stay. And the fol
lowing day—after he'd returned to hospital and discovered tha
the reason why his hand still hurt was because he'd broken it—
he'd found himself a bedsit where the landlord accepted cas
and asked no questions.

'So you ended up owning half the market, did you?' Sar
asked.

'No. It was the start of the Internet revolution. I found some
one who could do me a website, someone else who coul
handle the postage and delivery side of things and a wholesale
who'd give me a bulk discount. It was a bit of a gamble, but i
paid off. The business went just the way I hoped it would.'

'You decided not to go to university, then?'

He shook his head. 'I wanted to be out in the real world
Making money instead of listening to other people talk abou
it.' That, and the fact that he hadn't sat his exams. With hi
writing hand broken, there hadn't been any point in eve
turning up for the papers. So he'd left school at fifteen withou

any formal qualifications. Which meant no A levels. Which meant no university.

Though Luke had always known that he wouldn't make it in the money markets. Not with his family background. Who would trust the son of a thief, the grandson of a fraudster? And quite how he'd managed to talk his way onto the MBA course where he'd met Karim, he'd never know.

'So you were a dot-com millionaire.'

'Yes.' He shrugged. 'And then I got bored.'

'And that's when you started buying failing businesses, to see if you could make them work again?'

He knew he should give her a one-word answer and change the subject. And yet...there was something about Sara. Something that encouraged him to talk. So, against his better judgement he told her. 'It was by accident, really. The gym I went to...I used to have a beer with the owner, from time to time.' A friend of his old boxing teacher—who'd lectured him like mad on the idiocy of bare-knuckle fighting and who'd said he needed to learn the discipline of martial arts instead. Anyway, Lin told me that the landlords were hiking the rent yet again and he wasn't going to be able to cover his costs, so he was having to sell up. I didn't want the hassle of finding another gym that suited me, so I talked him into letting me have a quick look at his books to see if I could do anything.' He smiled. 'I could see the problems, and I managed to fix them. In return, Lin gave me a free pass to the gym and taught me kick-boxing.'

'Kick-boxing? Isn't that...well, violent?'

'Not if it's done properly. It's controlled and disciplined.'

'Like you.'

'Like me,' he agreed. 'Best thing ever if you've had a bad day and you want to get rid of the stress.'

'By kicking hell out of someone, you mean?'

'No.' That was what certain members of his family had done. Maybe even still did. Another reason why he didn't want anything to do with their life, ever. 'Kick-boxing's fast-paced, but it's *controlled*. And the discipline you learn from it helps with other sports.'

'So you're a sports freak.'

'What do you expect from a guy who owns several health clubs?' he asked mildly. 'I play squash a couple of times a week, I do kick-boxing a couple of times a week and I do some training in the machine room the rest of the time.'

She groaned. 'Don't tell me—and you never miss a sporting event on television.'

'Actually, I don't have a television.'

She stared at him, looking surprised for a moment. 'Let me guess. You don't bother watching because you'd rather spend the time working.'

'Got it in one.'

'But don't you…? Well, you must do something to relax.'

'I do.' It often involved a party with some fairly tedious conversation, followed by hot sex. He even considered telling her so, just to see if it would shock her. 'Sometimes I go and see a band. Dinosaur rock, as you'd have it. You can't beat it when it's really loud.'

'What about the cinema? The theatre?'

'Not really my cup of tea.'

Then, to his relief, the traffic started moving. 'About time, too,' he commented. He glanced at the clock on the dashboard. 'We're going to be about an hour late. But it'll still be early enough to eat.' And from now on he'd keep the conversation to safe topics. Such as work.

CHAPTER FIVE

AT FIVE past eight, Luke pulled up in the hotel car park. Sara schooled her face into neutral as she looked at the building. The paint was peeling off the stucco and the woodwork; she had to remind herself that seaside buildings always looked scruffy because of the salt content in the air. And maybe the place would be better inside, less run-down.

But her hopes faded as they walked into reception.

'I'm sorry, there's been a problem.' The receptionist looked ready to burst into tears when Luke started to check in. 'We had a burst pipe this afternoon and we can't put you in the rooms you booked.'

'Not to worry. We don't mind taking two different rooms,' Luke said.

The receptionist bit her lip. 'That's the thing. The water damage…it means we only have one room left. A double.'

Sara stared at her in horror. Surely the girl wasn't suggesting that they should *share* a room?

But that seemed to be precisely what she was saying.

'Luke. We need to talk,' she said in an urgent whisper, nudging his arm.

He let her lead him away from the desk. 'What?'

'We can't share a room. We'll have to go somewhere else.'

'At this time on a Friday night in the middle of summer, we'll be lucky to find anywhere else.'

'There must be *somewhere*.'

Luke rolled his eyes. 'For pity's sake, Sara. We've been stuck in the car for the last six hours. Right now all I want to do is eat, have a shower, check my emails and sleep. OK, so we didn't plan on sharing a room. But it's only for one night. We're adults and we're colleagues and we're perfectly capable of sharing a room without having sex.'

She wasn't so sure. 'Uh-huh.'

He sighed. 'Look, I'm not going to leap on you.'

There was no answer to that. And she couldn't exactly tell him she thought it was more likely that she'd leap on *him*. So she said nothing.

He clearly misread her silence, because he closed his eyes briefly. 'Before you say it, it's not because I think you're unattractive either, because you are. And telling you you're attractive doesn't mean I'm going to try making a move on you.' He shook his head. 'Why do women have to be so bloody *complicated*?'

He meant *needy*, she knew. She lifted her chin. 'I'm not complicated.'

'I'm not in the mood for an argument. I'm tired and I want a shower and something to eat. We'll cope. Look, I'll ask for an extra duvet or something and I'll sleep on the floor.'

'Uh-huh.'

He walked back over to the reception desk. 'Thanks. We'll take the room,' he said.

Sara simply followed him when he pocketed the room key and picked up both their cases.

The room was even worse than she'd feared. Small, with only just enough room for the bed, one narrow bedside table, a built-in wardrobe and a chest of drawers. No way was there enough space for him to sleep on the floor. They'd have to share the bed.

'Don't say a thing,' he warned, dumping their cases on the bed. 'Right now, my first priority is food.'

The meal turned out to be as awful as the room. Apart from

he fact it took ages to arrive, her grilled chicken was so dry it
asted like ashes, the sauce was decidedly gloopy and the veg-
tables were soggy. His food clearly wasn't much better,
ecause he picked at it and finally pushed his plate away.

'Maybe everything seems so bad because we've had a rotten
ourney,' she said. 'Maybe everything will seem better tomorrow.'

'Maybe.' He didn't look convinced. 'Right now, the only
hing this place has going for it is the staff.'

A receptionist who'd gone into panic mode, a cook who—
well, couldn't—and a waitress who'd whispered at them.

But that wasn't fair. For all she knew, the burst pipe had
ffected the kitchen as well. Perhaps the cook had had a lousy
ay and this wasn't the normal standard of the food here.

Even so, surely Luke wasn't really intending to buy this place?

On the other hand, he'd said how much he liked turning
ound businesses that were in a mess. This one definitely
eemed a mess, and it was just the sort of challenge she had a
eeling he'd love.

'Right. I need a shower and I want to check my emails.'

And then…they'd be going to bed.

Together.

Her mouth went dry.

As he'd said, they were adults. They were perfectly capable
f sleeping in the same room—the same bed—without having
ex. But even so she felt the adrenalin flooding through to her
ngertips as she followed Luke to their room.

He opened the door and stood aside, letting her through
rst. And then her stomach rumbled. Really loudly.

She grimaced. 'Sorry.'

'Not your fault.' He shrugged. 'We could go and find the
earest fast-food place.'

True, but she also knew he was tired. Just as she would be,
ad she spent six solid hours driving. 'I've got a better idea.
Iang on a sec.' She rummaged in her suitcase and produced a
arge bar of chocolate. 'My emergency stash.'

'You carry emergency chocolate?' He looked amused.

'Don't knock it.'

'I wouldn't dream of it.' He sat on the bed and gratefull took the large piece she broke off for him. 'This is good stuff. he said after the first taste. 'Thanks.' He smiled ruefully. 'I'm sorry I've dragged you into this. The hotel wasn't meant to b this bad. A bit run-down—shabby genteel, that's what th agent told me.'

'Sexing it up.' Oh, hell. She really shouldn't have said tha word. Sara avoided Luke's gaze. 'I mean, it might look bette in the morning.'

'I don't think so, somehow.' He paused. 'Do you want th first shower while I check my emails?'

'Thanks.'

At least the water was hot. But there weren't any compli mentary toiletries; Sara was glad she'd thought to bring showe gel with her.

Though there was nothing she could do about her pyjamas a little strappy top and cropped trousers which emphasised he curves. Still, she'd worked out very quickly that Luke was man of honour; she could trust his word.

Whether she could trust herself was another matter.

He was sitting on the edge of the bed, rapidly typing on hi laptop, when she emerged from the bathroom. He glanced u at her. 'That's the first time I've seen your hair down.'

She usually wore it up for work.

'I like it,' he added. 'Given that I know your low opinio of high-maintenance women, dare I ask if you use straighten ers on it?'

'It's naturally like this.' She smiled wryly. 'Dead straigh And I used to hate it when I was younger. I used to go to be in plaits, even though they were uncomfortable.'

'All for the sake of curls? You needn't have bothered.'

'I know. They usually fell out by the time I'd had breakfast

'That isn't what I meant—I was trying to pay you a compli

ment. It suits you like that.' Then he scanned her from top to toe. 'I'm glad one of us has something to sleep in.'

Sara felt her eyes widen. 'What do you mean?'

'I don't normally bother. And, as I wasn't expecting to share a room with you, I don't have any pyjamas with me.' He smiled wryly. 'Actually, I don't think I even possess a pair.'

She could well believe it. And the idea of sleeping next to him while he was completely naked... Her face felt hot, so she guessed that she'd blushed deeply. Really obviously.

He lifted a shoulder. 'Don't worry, Sara. I'll make myself decent so I won't embarrass you. I'm going to have a shower.' He climbed off the bed. 'Choose which side you want. I'm not fussy.'

When Luke came out of the bathroom a few minutes later, wearing just a pair of jersey boxer shorts, Sara had arranged herself in bed, on the side with the light and the bedside table, and was busily studying a puzzle magazine. She just hoped that Luke didn't look over her shoulder at the page, or he'd see that she was filling in the answers randomly—and she knew he was sharp enough to work out that it was because her concentration was shot to pieces.

His skin was still damp from his shower, his hair was tousled and he looked utterly edible. Her pulse rate went up several notches.

'The shower was freezing,' he remarked.

Guilt flooded through her. 'Sorry. I didn't realise I'd used all the hot water.'

'In a hotel, you're not supposed to be able to use all the hot water,' he reminded her.

'Maybe it's to do with the burst pipe. I never thought about it.'

He spread his hands. 'No matter. It's probably just as well. I needed a cold shower anyway.'

Her nipples tightened. Was he saying he was just as attracted to her and needed to cool his desire? And he'd said earlier that he thought she was attractive...

She didn't dare meet his gaze, just made a noncommittal murmur and continued pretending to do her puzzle.

As he climbed into bed beside her, the mattress dipped under his weight. He shifted, then shifted again, turned his pillow over and shifted yet again.

'I've changed my mind about shabby genteel,' he said crossly. 'This place is just *shabby*. The mattress is lumpy, too.'

Sara couldn't help laughing.

'What?' he demanded.

'Complaining about the mattress. Isn't it meant to be the princess and the pea, not the prince and the pea?' she teased.

'Very funny.' But then, as she lowered her puzzle book to glance at him, he smiled wryly at her. 'Ah, ignore me, Sara. I'm tired and grumpy. I'm going to get some sleep. Goodnight.'

'Goodnight.'

He turned so that his back was to her. She pretended to do a couple more clues, then closed the book and switched off the bedside light. But she couldn't sleep; she lay awake in the darkness, aware that Luke's body was very close to hers and that he was wearing very, very little.

And it was oh, so tempting to turn on her side and curl into him. Slide her arm round his waist and press her cheek against his back, absorbing the warmth of his body—despite the fact that it was the middle of summer, the night had a distinct chill to it.

And if she cuddled in to him, what then? Would he lace his fingers through hers? Or would he turn so that he was facing her, holding her close to his heart? Would he dip his head, steal a kiss?

She knew there was an attraction between them. One neither of them had acted on, because they were being sensible and businesslike and adult about things. But she also knew that there was no reason why they couldn't act on that attraction. They were both free, both single.

Except...

After Hugh, Sara had promised herself she would only get

involved with a man who'd commit to her. A man who'd put her before his job.

Luke Holloway wasn't that kind of man. He was a self-confessed workaholic who got bored easily. Who thrived on change. Who hadn't committed to any of his previous girl-friends—his relationships lasted a matter of weeks. Given the little he'd told her about his past, she was pretty sure he had huge barriers in place to make sure nobody came too close.

No, Luke wasn't Mr Right.

And she'd do well to remember that.

She heard his breathing deepen and become regular; he was clearly asleep. And then Sara, too, turned on her side with her back to him, relaxed and allowed herself to drift off.

The following morning, Sara was aware of light filtering through the curtains. Drowsily, she started to open her eyes—and then she realised where she was.

In bed with Luke Holloway.

But not as she'd gone to sleep last night, with her back facing his.

No, somehow, in the night, they'd moved into each other's arms. Her head was on his shoulder, her leg was draped over both of his, her hand was curled intimately round his inner thigh and her fingers were resting under the hem of his boxer shorts. Against his bare skin.

Which meant there were just a couple of millimetres between her fingers and his erect penis.

Oh, no.

She was practically *groping* him.

How on earth could she possibly face him?

The one good thing was that his breathing was even and regular and deep; clearly Luke was still asleep. If she could just move her leg without waking him, remove her hand from its intimate position and wriggle out of his arms, she could rescue the situation.

She'd just started to move, very carefully and very gently, when she became aware of a rumble of laughter in his chest. And his voice was full of amusement when he said, 'So Sleeping Beauty wakes at last…'

CHAPTER SIX

MORTIFYING.

This was utterly, utterly *mortifying*.

Luke had been awake all the time—and he'd been well aware of exactly where her hands were.

'Have you been awake long?' she asked, silently praying that the answer would be no.

It wasn't.

'Long enough,' he said.

Worse and worse. So he must have been lying there for ages. And the situation must be just as awkward for him: after all, he was the one being draped over. Being groped. Hastily, she shifted so she was no longer sprawled over him and removed her hand. 'I'm sorry. Um…Luke, I didn't mean to…' Her voice faded and she could feel her face heating.

'I know you didn't. And I don't mind.'

But she did. She was practically squirming with embarrassment.

'It's a little more than not minding,' he said softly. 'Actually, I liked having your hands on me.' He drew his free hand down her side, moulding his palm to her curves. 'And I like having my hands on you, too.'

She dragged in a breath. 'I thought you said…' That they could be adult about it. That they could share a room—a bed—without having sex.

'That was last night. This is now. Different day, different viewpoint.' He gave her a wicked grin. 'And I could point out that I wasn't the person with one leg sprawled over you and my hand up your pyjamas.'

This time, she did squirm. 'That's a bit below the belt.'

His grin widened. 'So was your hand.'

Oh, help. This was getting worse and worse.

He shifted so that he was facing her. He still had one arm wrapped round her, holding her close to him; his cornflower blue eyes were lazy and sexy and irresistible.

'Good morning,' he said softly.

'Good morning.' She just about managed to get the words out; right now, with that hot, sexy expression in his eyes, she could barely breathe. Even though she knew it wasn't physically possible, desire seemed to have taken the place of oxygen in her lungs.

He dipped his head slightly and kissed the tip of her nose. 'Sara.'

This was tempting. Incredibly tempting. She could see in his face what he wanted.

The same thing that *she* wanted.

Though if they gave in to their mutual urge and made love, it would make their working relationship seriously awkward.

'We shouldn't do this,' she warned, her voice shaky.

He stroked her face. 'I know. This is a seriously bad idea. I should have more self-control.'

'We've only known each other for a couple of weeks,' she pointed out.

'That's long enough. I already know you. You're bossy.'

'Bossy?'

'Yeah, but I forgive you because you're good at what you do and you're good to work with.' He stole a brief kiss. 'You love the colour pink. You're a history nut, you like girly films and the theatre, you believe everyone's nice, you're mad enough to enjoy filing, you play the piano and you have a thing about ice cream and paddling in the sea. What else do I need to know?'

'Nothing, I suppose.' She bit her lip. 'I know hardly anything about you. Just that you're a hotshot businessman who hates clutter. You like posh chocolate biscuits, you take your coffee black with one sugar, you do kick-boxing and squash and you never watch television. You listen to dinosaur rock, and you have a seriously expensive taste in cars. That's not a lot, Luke.'

'There isn't much more to me than that.'

'I'm sure there is.'

'Shallow as a puddle, that's me.'

'Like hell. You're more like still waters running deep.'

'Still.' He tested the word. 'Hmm. Interesting. I don't think anyone's ever said that about me before. And I'm not sure whether it goes with the other description you use for me—workaholic.'

'All right, so you live your life at a hundred miles an hour and I'm mixing my metaphors,' she said crossly.

'I've just thought of something else about you. You talk too much and there's only one way I can think of to shut you up.'

She lifted her chin. 'That's so corny.'

'True, though. The only thing I can think about right now. Kissing you. Touching you.'

'That's two things.'

He groaned. 'I mean it. I really want to kiss you.' He moistened his lower lip. 'I've wanted you for *days*, Sara—probably since the moment you walked into my office and started bossing me about.'

It was the same for her. The moment she'd seen him with his feet up on the desk, talking on the phone, his hair sexily rumpled. Which was why she'd let him talk her into staying longer, being his temporary PA, instead of just finishing the trouble-shooting job and moving on to the next client. 'Me, too,' she admitted.

'So there's a pretty logical conclusion here.' He traced her lower lip with his thumb and Sara's lips automatically parted.

'I'm so glad you agree with me,' he said softly and bent his head to kiss her. His mouth brushed against hers, the contact light and teasing and tempting her to respond. When she tipped her head back slightly, he deepened the kiss, offering and demanding at the same time.

Sara had kissed men before. Been to bed with men before. But this… This was something else. The feel of Luke's mouth against hers made every nerve-end tingle, made her blood feel as if it were fizzing through her veins.

His fingers slid under the hem of her pyjama top. He stroked her waist, the pads of his fingertips brushing against her skin, and she shivered, wanting more. Taking the invitation, he let his hand slide slowly up her body until he cupped one breast. His thumb rubbed across her hardened nipple, which suddenly felt supersensitive to his touch. A touch that wasn't enough for her. She needed more.

He broke the kiss. 'Do you like that?' he asked softly.

'Mmm.' She couldn't quite manage a proper word.

'Then how about this?' He shimmied down the bed and, to her shock, he opened his mouth over her nipple, sucking her through her pyjama top. A pulse started to beat rapidly between her thighs and she couldn't help sliding her fingers through his hair, urging him on.

'I'll take that as a yes,' he whispered, and bunched her top upwards. He nuzzled his way over her stomach, pausing to tease her with the tip of his tongue circling her navel, and then at last, at last, closed his mouth over one nipple. Without the thin jersey of her top in the way, it was even better: the teasing flick of his tongue, the pressure of his lips and the light graze of his teeth against her nipple made her arch against him in pleasure.

And then he slid his hands between her thighs, cupping her through her pyjama bottoms. He rocked his hand, so the base of his thumb rubbed against her clitoris, and she couldn't hold back a whimper of longing. 'Luke.'

He kissed her mouth, hard, then hooked his fingers into the

waistband of her pyjama bottoms and started to pull them down. She raised her hips, letting him pull the material clear, and shivered as he kissed his way down her thighs, caressing every millimetre of skin as he uncovered it.

And then her breath hitched as he worked his way back up again. He paused at the hollows of her ankles, and again at the backs of her knees. By the time he reached her inner thighs, Sara was shaking; gently, he eased her thighs further apart and knelt between them. She couldn't open her eyes; all she could do was whisper, 'Luke, you're driving me crazy.'

'That's the idea.' His voice sounded husky, sensual and sexy as hell.

She wriggled in anticipation, and heard him laugh softly. And then, at last, he drew a finger along her sex—and then all the way back again.

'Please,' she whispered.

He did it again. And again. And then he shifted slightly and she felt his breath against her skin. She held her breath, waiting, willing him to do it. And when she felt the slow stroke of his tongue, she shuddered and fisted her hands in his hair again.

'You taste so sweet,' he whispered against her skin.

In response, she tilted her pelvis.

She felt him shift back slightly. Surely he wasn't going to stop now? She screwed her eyes shut and tipped her head back against the pillows. 'I can't believe you're going to stop now.'

'I'm not intending to stop.'

'Then what?' She opened her eyes and stared at him.

'I'm just checking that you're sure you know what you're doing.'

'Of course I do.'

'Because, if you look at this logically, as you said, this is a seriously bad idea.'

True. Though, right now, stopping felt like an even worse idea.

Maybe she'd spoken the words aloud, or maybe he'd just read

it in her expression, because he simply said, 'Yeah, it's the same for me.' Then he took her hand and curled it round his erection.

She tightened her grip and rocked her hand slightly, wanting to tease him the way he'd teased her, and he groaned. 'Sara. I can't think straight now. All I want to do is bury myself in you. Deep.'

'Then do it,' she said, 'because I'm going to…to *implode* if you don't carry on.' And, just to make sure he got the message, she tightened her thumb and forefinger round his shaft again and drew the circle slowly up and down.

Just once.

He swallowed hard. 'I need a condom. Now.' He vaulted out of bed, and Sara realised that he must have taken his boxer shorts off at the same time as he'd removed her pyjama bottoms. Naked, Luke was glorious—completely unselfconscious and gorgeous. His body was sculpted and perfectly toned.

And the way he moved, graceful and sure as a dancer, turned her on even more.

He retrieved a condom from his wallet and returned to the bed.

Then it hit her that he carried condoms in his wallet. And how many names she'd seen his linked with.

'Do you do this a lot?' she asked.

'What?'

'Sleep with your staff.'

'Never.' He looked serious. 'It's an unbreakable rule.'

One he was about to break?

As if he'd read her mind, he said softly, 'Strictly speaking, you're not my staff. You're my consultant. You're your own boss.'

'I think you're splitting hairs.'

He reached over and wound the end of her hair round his fingers. 'Mmm. You have lovely hair. I wanted to do this last night. Except I was tired and grumpy and I wouldn't have made it good for you.'

She shivered. 'And you're intending to make it good for me now?'

'Sara, I've barely started.'

She knew she should leave it there, but this nagging voice in her head wouldn't let up. 'So you're good at this. You get a lot of practice.'

He sighed. 'Without being arrogant, yes, I tend to be good at things I like doing.'

Like making love.

'And yes to the practice—in the past. I haven't had a lot of time lately, so I haven't seen anyone for a while.'

Which didn't answer her real question.

Her thoughts must have shown on her face, because he stroked her cheek with the backs of his fingers. 'But I know what you're really asking, so I'll tell you. I date a lot, but I'm fussy. Whatever you might read in the gossip columns, I don't sleep with just anything in a skirt.'

He leaned down and brushed his mouth against hers. 'Stop thinking. Just *feel*.' He looked at her and hooked one finger under the strap of her pyjama top, easing it down over her shoulder. The top he'd pushed up earlier to bare her breasts. 'I like this. A lot. But it has to go: I want you skin to skin.'

She couldn't quite get past the implications of what he'd said. 'You have a lot of sex.'

He sighed. 'Sara, I like sex. I like good sex. And, yes, I like lots of it. But, as I told you, I'm fussy.' He paused. 'One thing I should be clear about, though. I'm not in the market for marriage and happy-ever-afters. So this is just you and me, here and now. It's not a declaration of intent, and it's not going to get in the way of work. It's just getting this craziness out of our systems so we can go back to normal and work together. Sara. I like you. I think you like me, or you wouldn't be working with me. Neither of us is seeing anyone else. So where's the problem?'

'Just so you know, I'm not looking for a relationship.'

'Fine.'

'And I'm not in the habit of sleeping around.'

He smiled. 'If it makes you feel better, I don't think you're a tart. That isn't why you're naked—well, almost naked—and in bed with me. That's…'

'…because the hotel's a mess and we had no alternative but to share a room?' she finished.

'I guess. Though I'd also say that it's serendipity. As I said, I've been having trouble keeping my hands off you. When I'm in the office, I keep looking over at you at the computer, and thinking about walking over to you and lifting you out of your chair and laying you on your desk and…' He slid one hand between her thighs again, his fingertips brushing her skin but staying millimetres away from her sex. 'Touching you. Tasting you. Easing my body into yours and making you come so hard that you forget where you are. Making you come until you scream with pleasure.'

The image flickered in her mind and her mouth went dry. 'Luke,' she whispered.

'I want to be inside you, Sara. Right now. And I think that's where you want me, too.' He moved his hand to cup her sex again. 'You feel hot.'

So hot that she was burning up. 'Yes.' She barely got the word out.

His fingertip skated over her clitoris, with just the right pressure and at just the right speed to push her pulse rate up another notch. She dragged in a breath, and it turned to a gasp of sheer pleasure as he pushed one finger inside her. 'And wet,' he said, his voice dropping an octave.

'Yes.'

'And ready for me.' He paused. 'Say it.'

'I'm ready for you.' Each word was punctuated with a dragged-in breath.

He withdrew his hand. 'Now, lose the top.'

She sat up; her fingers were shaking as she pulled the top over her head. And she felt suddenly shy; even though her hair was long, it wasn't long enough to cover her breasts. And she was sitting there in front of Luke, completely naked. Practically displaying herself to him.

He twirled the ends of her hair round his fingers again. 'You're gorgeous, Sara Fleet. You turn me on—in a big way.'

'All words and no action, Mr Holloway?' Her voice was raspy, but she was determined to give as good as she got—not to be all shy and embarrassed, even though she felt it.

He gave her a wolfish smile. 'I'm going to make you take that back, Ms Fleet. I'm going to make you beg.' He ripped the foil packet open and rolled the condom onto his penis.

'Is that a threat?'

'A promise,' he corrected, his blue eyes glittering with desire.

This time, his kiss was hotter. More demanding. It made her head spin, and then he eased his hand between her legs again, stroking and teasing until her whole body felt hot, almost molten.

'Luke,' she whispered.

In answer, he pushed his finger into her. Very, very slowly. So slowly that it drove her crazy. She tightened her internal muscles round him, and he smiled.

'Anything you want to say to me?' he teased.

She narrowed her eyes at him. 'You *know* what.'

'I'm not a mind-reader,' he added, his eyes glittering. 'Say it.'

'I want you,' she said. 'Inside me.'

He'd said he was going to make her beg. If he made her wait any longer, she'd go crazy. 'Please, Luke.'

He smiled and fitted the tip of his sheathed penis against her sex, and slowly, slowly eased in. He stayed there for a moment, letting her get used to the feel of him, and then she wrapped her legs round his waist, urging him deeper.

Taking his weight on his arms, he dipped down to brush his mouth against hers; she opened her mouth under his and he responded with a kiss that demanded and gave in equal measure.

This man, she thought, could be addictive. Because he paid attention to detail—he noted the change in her breathing when a particular touch or caress excited her, and repeated it until she was quivering and spiralling out of control.

The lumpy mattress was forgotten. All she could focus on

was the way Luke made her feel, the sensation of his body moving inside her and the touch of his skin against hers.

And just as her orgasm hit, he held her closer, murmuring her name over and over like a litany; she could tell from the way his body tensed that he, too, had reached his climax.

When the aftershocks of pleasure died away, he withdrew carefully, moved onto his back and shifted so that he was holding her close. Neither of them spoke; she was happy just to feel the beat of his heart against her cheek.

'I need to deal with something,' he said eventually, stroking her hair. 'Excuse me a moment.'

But as he moved from the bed and she heard water running the spell broke and she thought about what they'd done. How stupid she'd been.

Her doubts must have shown on her face because he raised an eyebrow on his return from the bathroom. 'What's up?'

'You're right—this was a bad idea. We work together.'

'We've been through this already. It's OK. Relax. We're both professionals, so this isn't going to interfere with work.' He kissed her lightly. 'I'll let you have the first shower. Though it had probably better not be with me, or we won't be out of here until well after lunchtime.'

Oh, the thought that put in her head. If she'd been standing up, her knees would've buckled.

'Go and have a shower,' he repeated. 'Then we're going to have breakfast, look round the hotel and discuss things over lunch.'

'OK.' She paused. 'Um, would you mind handing me my pyjamas? Or closing your eyes?'

'It's a bit late for that. We've seen each other up close and very personal.' He kissed the tip of her nose. 'But if it makes you happy…' He retrieved her pyjamas and handed them to her. 'I'll sit with my back to you and my eyes closed, OK?'

He obviously thought she was being ridiculous—and she probably was, given how intimately they'd explored each other's bodies—but at least he'd humoured her. 'Thank you.' She put

er pyjamas back on again, retrieved her clothes from the
ardrobe and dresser and locked the bathroom door behind her.

She'd have a shower. Wash her hair. And maybe she could
redge up some common sense in the middle of it all.

CHAPTER SEVEN

WHEN Sara emerged from the bathroom, fully dressed, Luke was sitting up in bed, covered by a sheet up to his waist, working on his laptop. There was a pile of clothes on the bed next to him; clearly he intended to follow her lead and put his clothes on with a closed door between them.

'The bathroom's all yours,' she said.

'Thanks.' He saved his file, switched off the laptop, then headed for the bathroom while Sara averted her gaze.

While he showered and dressed, she busied herself tidying the room. Putting the bed back into a semblance of decency and trying not to think about just how she and Luke had rumpled the sheets only a few minutes before.

'Shall we go down to breakfast?' he asked as he came out of the bathroom.

His hair was damp and tousled and he looked thoroughly gorgeous, but his tone was casual and neutral. As if they were colleagues who'd had separate rooms and he'd merely knocked on her door at the agreed time. As if they hadn't just blown each other's minds.

She suppressed the throb of disappointment. This was how she'd wanted it, wasn't it? 'Sure. Is that your idea of casual?' She indicated his formal trousers and crisp white shirt.

'I'm not wearing a tie.' He shrugged. 'How else am I going to dress?'

'We're at the seaside. You can't paddle in trousers; you need shorts.'

'No, I don't. Besides, shorts don't exactly go with shoes.'

Especially as his were highly polished and looked handmade. Though he'd look great in shorts. The sort that came down to the knees—cut-off black chinos, with that white shirt unbuttoned a little more and his sleeves rolled up a bit. Add a pair of dark glasses and bare feet, and he'd be stunning. Like a pirate.

'Unlike some people around here,' he added, clearly oblivious to the thoughts running through her head, 'I don't have the contents of half a shoe shop in my wardrobe.'

'I don't have that many pairs.' Not with her, at any rate.

'You've worn seven different pairs to the office already. And the ones you're wearing right now are different again.'

He'd noticed her shoes?

She wasn't quite sure what to think. In her experience, men didn't notice shoes. Then again, Luke was the kind of man who could make you think he was wool-gathering, but would get ten out of ten if you told him to close his eyes and then asked him detailed questions about his surroundings.

'You don't wear shoes when you paddle,' she said.

'I'm not buying a pair of shorts just to please you.'

She shrugged. 'Your choice. You'll just have to roll your trousers up to your knees.'

'I'm not going…' His voice faded and he held both hands up in surrender. 'OK. I submit. Otherwise you'll argue with me until breakfast is over—and I'm starving.'

They went down to the hotel restaurant together. Clearly they were here towards the end of the hotel's allotted time for the meal, because only one other table was occupied—and the elderly couple looked as if they'd almost finished their meal. There was a help-yourself cold buffet set out on tables at one end of the room, or the menu stated that they could order a full English breakfast. Remembering their meal from the previous evening, Sara decided to go for the safe option, sticking to fruit and yoghurt. Luke was clearly thinking along the same lines as he opted for toast.

The coffee, when it arrived, was stewed. Maybe it was their fault for arriving so late, she thought, but did it really take that much effort to make half a pot of fresh coffee? And when she glanced at Luke's plate, she noticed that the butter hadn't melted into his toast. Which meant it was probably cold and chewy, like the stuff she remembered from her student days. She wasn't surprised when he left most of it.

'So what's the plan for this morning?' she asked.

'Look around. Mental notes. Actually, there's a spa here, so you could go for a treatment.'

'What sort of treatment?'

He spread his hands. 'Anything you like. My bill. And before you protest,' he added with a grin, 'I can't exactly try out myself, can I?'

'There's no reason why men can't have a facial.'

He groaned. '*Please.* Do you talk to your brother like this?'

She thought about it. 'Yes. Both of them.'

'Just book something,' he said. 'And I'm going to use the hotel pool.'

Ten minutes later, she texted him. *Beautician fully booked. Going for a walk on the beach. Call me when you're ready.*

Almost immediately, her phone rang.

'I'm ready now,' Luke said, 'so I might as well take that walk with you.'

'I thought you were going for a swim?'

'The pool's out of action because of the burst pipe,' he said. 'So I think we need a discussion over coffee.'

'Provided it's somewhere else,' she said in a low voice. 'This morning's was undrinkable. I could really, really do with a latte.'

'Does this mean you don't want lunch here, either?'

'I've got a better idea. We skip lunch and have an ice cream on the beach.'

He sighed. 'You're going to nag until you get it, aren't you?'

'Absolutely. And my paddle in the sea—*our* paddle,' she corrected herself.

'Where are you?'

'Reception.'

'Stay put. I'll meet you there.'

He joined her in a couple of minutes and they headed towards the seafront. They found a small café overlooking the sea where the coffee smelled good and the scent of bacon was mouth-watering.

True to form, her stomach rumbled.

Luke stifled a grin, but not before she noticed. 'Emergency chocolate required?' he asked.

'An emergency bacon sandwich would be better.'

'That,' Luke said, 'is the second-best idea you've had this morning.'

Was the first making love with him? Though she wasn't sure she dared ask.

'Find us a table—I'll go and order. Latte, wasn't it?'

'Thanks.'

He joined her, carrying the coffee. When the bacon sandwich arrived, the bread was thickly cut from a bloomer loaf, incredibly soft and fresh; the bacon was home-cured and grilled to the perfect crispness, and the tomato ketchup definitely tasted home-made.

'This,' she said after finishing her first mouthful, 'is fantastic. And this is what that hotel should've been offering this morning. I bet you anything you like, their bacon would've been microwaved and their bread would've been soggy.'

'You're really not impressed with the hotel, are you?' Luke asked wryly.

'Let's face it, they don't have a clue. And if you really need me to list what's wrong...'

'Go for it,' he invited.

It took her eight minutes.

'You're absolutely right,' he said when she'd finished.

'But?' She could see the word in his face.

'But doesn't that feel like a challenge for you?' he asked 'Doesn't it make you want to go and sort it all out?'

She sighed. 'I know you like a challenge, Luke, but I think th place needs too much work. And it's probably listed—so you' end up going through tons of red tape if you want to do so muc as painting a window frame, let alone anything structural.'

He raised an eyebrow. 'So you're an expert on listed buildings?

'My family home's listed,' she explained, 'so I know fror work my parents have had done in the past that it can be a night mare. Luckily we know this brilliant architect, Max Taylor, wh specialises in restoring listed buildings. And he's got fantasti contacts—that saves a huge amount of time. He tells us exactl what needs to be done and who can do it, and the local plannin department know he knows what he's doing so they trust hir and don't drag things out.'

'He sounds like a very useful contact. Perhaps you can intro duce me to him.'

'Sure. But I can tell you now he won't come all the way uj here,' she warned. 'Unless it's a really special building—whic that hotel most definitely isn't—he only works within the are of the M25.'

Luke frowned. 'I thought your family lived in Kent.'

'We do. Anyway, that doesn't include us.' She flapped a dis missive hand. 'We were clients before.'

'Before what?'

'Before he got married and had kids. He's a really hands on father.'

'I see.'

Although his expression hardly changed, she was aware tha there was a barrier between them. His eyes might just as wel have had steel shutters pulled down; she had absolutely no ide what he was thinking. What had she said to produce that effec so quickly?

Then she remembered what Luke had said about not havin a mother and her own supposition about the men in his family

looked as if she was right; Luke clearly had issues about
milies. And, if she didn't want him to clam up on her com-
etely, she needed to get their conversation back on track—
ito something he found safe. Work. 'Anyway. I don't think
s viable because it would take up all your time. It'd be closed
r months while you made the repairs and alterations, so you'd
e losing money hand over fist.'

Luke smiled. 'I think my cash flow would be able to with-
and it.'

She rolled her eyes. 'Of course. I forgot. You're a million-
re. That's why you're looking at buying a truly awful run-
wn place.'

'It's calling speculating to accumulate. And I did warn you
wasn't going to be luxurious,' he reminded her.

'A place can still be comfortable without costing an arm and
leg,' she pointed out. 'I don't doubt that you could do it.' Luke
olloway was the kind of man who could do anything he set
s mind to. 'But is it going to be worth the cost? And I don't
ean just financially.'

'My time, you mean?'

'And your social life. Either you'll have to fly from here to
ondon—that is, if there's an airport nearby—and that'll scupper
ur plans about being green, or you'll have to give up the parties.'

He shrugged. 'As I said before, I'm getting bored with the
irties.'

And bored with his gorgeous, exotic-looking model-type
rlfriends?

She pushed the thought away. It was irrelevant. He'd already
ade it clear that he wasn't looking for a relationship. What had
ppened between them this morning was clearly a one-off.

And she wasn't even going to let herself think about tonight.

'Have you thought about your clients?' she asked. 'Are they
ing to be local, or would you expect people to travel five
urs from London?'

'That's something to think about,' he said. 'But, as I said,

I'm looking to build a chain. All in spa towns and seasid resorts, like this. All with good, simple food cooked with loc ingredients. Old-fashioned good service and spa treatments— I could even offer genuine local spa waters, just as people too them a hundred years ago.'

She stared at him, horrified. 'Luke, have you ever actuall tasted spa water?'

'Have you?' he countered.

'Yes. And it's vile. Anyway, I thought spa therapy mea bathing in the stuff, not just drinking it?'

'Depends if the water's warm or cold,' Luke said. 'Or ho

Suddenly the heat was back in his eyes. And she had feeling that the idea inside her head matched the one inside hi just the two of them and a hot tub. Her hand was shakin slightly as she lifted her mug of latte; she really hoped l couldn't see it. Didn't guess what kind of effect he had on he

She really had to get a grip. Even if Luke was changing h mind about a relationship, she wasn't. 'Right. Enough work fe now. I want my walk on the beach,' she said, forcing herself sound all bright and chirpy, and not in the slightest as if sl wanted to drag him back to their awful hotel room and rip his clothes off.

'And the whippy ice cream with a chocolate flake in it. Yea yeah. I get the message.'

As they walked across the beach, Luke saw a man teaching h small son how to fly a kite.

More than twenty years ago, Luke had stood on this se same beach, doing exactly what the little boy was doing no giving every scrap of attention to the man who was holding t reel of string and explaining how to hold it. His father.

Sara clearly noticed what he was looking at, because sl asked softly, 'Did you ever do that as a kid?'

He nodded. 'I remember having a blue kite, the tradition shape with a really long red and yellow tail. Actually, it was

s beach my dad taught me to fly it. I must have been about
ır or five at the time. I couldn't keep the tension and the kite
ɔt dropping out of the sky, but he didn't give up. He rescued
nd brushed the wet sand off, and we kept going until finally
lew and I could feel the wind tugging at it. And it was so
ɔd to see my kite flying up there and knowing I was doing
ll myself…' He shook his head. 'Ah, it was a long time ago.
t important.'

She curled her fingers round his. 'Memories help to make
ı who you are.'

'Even the bad ones?' The words were out before he could
p them. Horrified, he shook his hand free. 'Forget I said that.'

'Even the bad ones,' she said, recapturing his hand, 'because
y teach you what you don't want out of life.'

Something in her voice alerted him. He looked at her, shaken
: of his own nightmare. 'That,' he said, 'sounds personal.'

'I've made some pretty bad decisions in the past. You know
at you said about me believing everyone's nice until proven
ıerwise?' At his nod she explained, 'I discovered someone
o wasn't so nice.'

He had a pretty good idea that the person in question was
le, and had hurt her badly. So he tightened his fingers briefly
ınd hers, to show her he understood and he sympathised
:hout pitying.

'But there's always a positive. Making that mistake hurt—
ɔt—but it helped me to realise what I don't want. And I won't
-eat my mistakes.'

Was that a warning? He needed to know. 'Was this morning
ıistake?' he asked softly.

'I don't know.'

At least she'd been honest with him. Even though it stung.

'Was it a mistake for you?' she asked.

He could see the vulnerability in her eyes. No way could he
' yes and hurt her. On the other hand, he had a feeling that,
spite their agreement that morning, Sara believed in happy-

ever-afters. Something he wasn't sure he could offer her. T
only thing he could do was to be honest. 'I don't know, eith
I didn't plan it to be like this.'

'Maybe,' she said, 'we both plan too much. Maybe
should just…see how things go.'

It shocked him that he was still holding her hand. It shock
him even more to realise that he didn't want to let it go. 'Ye
Though it might be a bit late for taking things slowly.'

Colour bloomed in her cheeks. And he wanted to kiss
all over again, lose himself in her. 'We'll see how things g
he said, and he kept his hand in hers.

As they reached the harbour, Sara nudged him and gestur
towards the chalked signs for boat trips.

He read them swiftly. 'You want to go out in the bay and s
the seals?'

'And the puffins,' she added with a smile. 'It's only for
hour and a half. I'll swap it for the paddle in the sea.'

'Feel free to go, if you want to. Though it's not my kind
thing.'

'Hey, if you're going into seaside hotels and leisure, you ne
to know what's on offer locally—so you can advise your gues

'If I'm not going to invest here, there isn't much point
scoping out the local facilities,' he pointed out.

'Ah, but you need a benchmark. Something by which y
can judge other operators. Besides, a bit of sea air will bl
the cobwebs away.'

He sighed. 'All right. If you insist, we'll go and see the sea

'Are you sure you can take sitting still and not using yo
mobile phone or sneaking in some work on a report—for all
an hour and a half?' she teased.

'No. But we'll do it, if it shuts you up about shorts a
paddling.'

She wasn't the slightest bit abashed. 'Good. Oh, and as t
is my idea, I'm paying.'

'Bu—'

'No arguments,' she cut in.

Well, OK. He was picking up the bill for everything else that weekend; if she wanted to do this, he wasn't going to refuse and make her feel bad. Even though it was far from his idea of being a treat. 'Thank you,' he said politely.

She bought the tickets, and their timing was perfect because the next trip was about to depart. There was just room enough for them in the boat, so he had to sit very close to her. And nearly everyone on the boat seemed to be in a family.

Well, he'd just have to live with it.

He pretended to be absorbed in the commentary. On the rocks, seals were basking in the sun. One rolled over and flapped a flipper, causing one of the children to yell that the seal was waving at him.

And even the seals were in family groups. The bull, large and protective, the cow, secure next to her mate, and the pup, settled happily and cuddled up to its parents.

Even though he usually avoided family situations as much as possible, part of him was charmed by the seals' huge dark eyes and almost spaniel-like faces. Some of the seals, more inquisitive than the others, made their cumbersome way into the water—and then suddenly they were gliding along, their heads bobbing up and disappearing and bobbing up again an impossible distance away.

He glanced at Sara. She was smiling; although her sunglasses hid the expression in her eyes, he'd bet they were all warm and soft. Right at that moment, she looked like a real English rose. And he really had to make an effort to stop himself pulling her close and kissing her.

'They're gorgeous, aren't they?' she asked.

'Yes,' he admitted.

Though he was glad she hadn't asked him if he was glad she'd pushed him into this. Because he really wasn't sure. Although the waters around them were so calm it was practically like a millpond, suddenly it felt as if he were sailing a tiny dinghy in high seas. Nothing was quite the same as it had been yesterday, and he couldn't put his finger on why he felt so thrown. Though he suspected it had something to do with her.

He listened to the crew's tales about the Old Horse Rocks and the seals, watched the puffins bobbing on the water, far tinier than he'd expected them to be, and then, as they sailed in close to the smugglers' coves, listened to tales of the rum-runners and pirates.

'You know, you'd look great as a pirate,' Sara said with a grin.

'I am *not* wearing shorts. Or an eye patch.'

'Arrr,' she mocked, in her best pirate impersonation, 'you're a chicken, you arrr.'

He just loved the way she teased him. And what was sauce for the goose… He bent his head so he could whisper into her ear. 'If you're asking me to play pirate tonight, honey, and rip your clothes off and ravish you, then it can be arranged.'

And he grinned when she blushed like a beacon.

Good. He was back in control of things again. And that was just how he liked it.

CHAPTER EIGHT

WHEN they reached dry land again, Sara said, 'So are you going to admit you enjoyed that?'

'The seals were cute. And the puffins.'

'But?'

Well, she'd asked him straight. He had to be honest. 'It's not really my kind of thing.' When she didn't say anything but the *why?* was clear in her expression, he sighed. 'Too many kids.'

'You don't like children?'

'My idea of hell,' he said, 'would be having to work in a nursery or a classroom. And be on playground duty.'

'You'd hate what my mum does, then—going out to local schools and telling them all about apples and old-fashioned Kentish recipes.'

'Mmm.' Not his scene at all.

'So you don't ever want children of your own?'

Absolutely not. He'd had a miserable childhood with a dad who hadn't been there half the time and a mum who had been physically present but too full of tranquillisers to notice anything. OK, so Luke wasn't his dad, but he wouldn't know how to begin to be a good father. And he had no intention of trying. 'Marriage and babies,' he said, 'are seriously overrated.'

'There's more to life than work.'

'True.' He shrugged. 'And there's more to life than babies.'

'Actually,' she said, 'babies are the point. Without them, the human race would die out.'

Trust her to zero in on that. 'I guess you're right. Someone has to produce children. But it's not going to be me.' A nasty realisation struck him. 'So you're looking for marriage and babies?'

'Not at the moment. But eventually, yes. When I meet the right person.'

'Mr Right? Do you really believe in all that hype?'

She spread her hands. 'My parents have been together for thirty-five years. My sister Louisa's happily married with a toddler. My brother Rupert's engaged. And I think Justin is seeing someone—though he's probably keeping it quiet because he knows that, the minute Lou finds out, she'll start planning his wedding.' She smiled. 'She has this terrible habit of matchmaking. She claims credit for three weddings and two engagements, excluding her own.'

Luke made a mental note to stay well away from Sara's sister.

He was being paranoid. His relationship with Sara was strictly business, or had been until this morning. Well. Physically, it had been strictly business. He'd been fantasising about Sara Fleet from the second he'd met her.

'Whatever floats your boat,' he said, aiming for cool. And he really wanted to stop talking about weddings and families. It was way, way outside his comfort zone. He glanced at his watch. 'I need to make a couple of calls, and I left the relevant paperwork back in the hotel. Do you mind?'

'No. Though I think I'll just go for a walk on the seafront. I might have that ice cream I've been promising myself.'

'Sure. I'll see you back at the room whenever you're ready.'

Though she didn't look too enthralled at the idea of going back to their hotel.

As he approached the place, he could see exactly what she meant. It wasn't genteel shabby at all. It was forlorn. The sunshine was unforgiving because it made the place look even worse.

Yet it had so much potential…

He shook himself. Forget the calls. They could wait. There was something else he needed to do first.

A couple of minutes on the Internet found him exactly the right place. A larger version of the sort of place he'd thought about turning his hotel into. Old-fashioned and yet with all mod cons. A place with a history and stunning views over the bay, and, better still, their best suite was free due to a last-minute cancellation.

He settled their bill at reception. 'Sorry, something cropped up and we have to leave,' he said. It was a fib, but the receptionist looked miserable so why make her day worse than it clearly already was? 'But of course I'll pay for tonight's room.'

He'd just finished packing their cases when Sara walked back in.

'What are you doing?' she asked, looking shocked.

'We're leaving.'

'What, now?' She glanced at her watch. 'At this rate we won't be back in London until ten o'clock—and that's if we don't stop on the way.'

'We're not going to London,' he explained. 'We're moving.'

'What?'

'I think we both deserve a non-lumpy mattress tonight.'

'And you just packed for us both.'

Was she going to have a hissy fit about the fact he'd packed her stuff? 'Yes, because it was quicker than waiting for you to get back, and I folded your stuff carefully. Let's go.'

Once Luke had made his mind up to do something, Sara thought, he didn't hang about. There was no point in discussing it further, so she simply followed him out to the car.

The hotel he'd booked was only a few minutes away and it was spotless from the outside. Perfect paintwork, without even the hint of a chip or a crack, the windows sparkled, and the car park at the back had tubs of summer flowers to brighten it up.

Inside, it was even better. Again, Luke refused to let her carry her case; when he'd picked up the key from the friendly, smiling receptionist, they took the lift to the top floor. Every surface was clean and, even in the lift, the carpet was so thick that you sank into it.

'Our suite,' Luke said, unlocking the door and ushering her in. 'Take a look around and see what you think.'

It was huge. A living room with comfortable sofas, a low coffee table and another table with a kettle and a selection of coffee, different kinds of tea and hot chocolate, plus fantastic biscuits. Another table held a beautiful display of fresh flowers. The French windows led onto a balcony with stunning views of Scarborough Bay—and she realised with pleasure that they'd actually be able to watch the sun set from there. There was a wrought-iron bistro table and two chairs on the balcony and another tub of the beautiful summer flowers like the ones in the car park.

There were two bathrooms, to her surprise, one with a power shower and one with a whirlpool bath. Complimentary toiletries, thick fluffy bath robes hanging on the door and plenty of room for spreading out.

Though there was only one bedroom. With an enormous bed, admittedly—but it was just *one* bed.

'This doesn't mean I'm expecting you to sleep with me,' Luke said softly from the doorway. 'I'll do the gentlemanly thing and sleep on the sofa, if you like.'

He was giving her the choice.

'It's a big bed,' she said.

'Super-king size, according to the girl on reception,' he told her.

'And we're perfectly capable of sharing it without...' Then she saw the smile on his face. 'What?'

'I was just remembering waking up this morning.' There was a distinct glitter in his eye. Amusement mixed with desire.

She felt her face heat. 'Um.'

His smile broadened. 'I don't mind sharing, if you don't.'

She was hardly in a position to protest. Especially as the suite was enormous, and he'd changed their hotel for her sake. 'I'm sorry. This must've cost a small fortune.'

He shrugged. 'It's not a problem.'

'Look, I ought to pay my share of it.'

'No. I'm the one who dragooned you into coming to Scarborough. So it's my bill. No arguments.'

'Then thank you.' She grimaced. 'I'm sorry I made such a fuss—I could've coped with another night in that other hotel, you know.'

'No, you couldn't. And neither could I.' He smiled wryly. 'You saw the "before". This is what I saw the place being "after".'

'And it's fabulous—but it'd take so much time and effort to make it like this. You'd really have to do a proper cost benefit analysis.'

'And a building survey and get quotes for the work that needs doing. True. But there's also my gut instinct.'

'Which is?'

'Usually right,' he said.

She groaned. 'That's infuriating. You know what I meant.'

'Be nice to me, or you'll be eating fish and chips on the harbour instead of a posh dinner,' he teased.

'There's nothing wrong with fish and chips. Anyway, I don't have the right clothes with me to have dinner in the restaurant here.' Her beige linen trousers and cream top and black loafers could pass muster as smart casual, but this was more a little black dress and strappy shoes sort of place.

'Actually,' he said, 'there's more than one restaurant—there's the formal dining room, and a café bar for something less formal. Pasta, pizza and burgers. But I was thinking room service. Dinner on the balcony, overlooking the sea and watching the sun set.' He proffered a menu. 'I checked this out online before I booked. It's pretty good.'

She scanned it quickly. 'I think I'll have to close my eyes and pick at random. This is just… Wow. I like *everything* on it. And it's all local produce. Organic, too.' She looked up at him. 'So this is the sort of thing you're planning to do?'

He nodded. 'Probably not on as big a scale as this. I like the idea of having a boutique hotel, maybe fifteen or twenty rooms. Small and exclusive.'

'Expanding to a chain.'

'Yup.'

And he'd do it, she knew. He'd find the right sort of place to change—somewhere a little less run-down than the hotel where they'd stayed the previous night, but a place that could still be transformed from something run-of-the-mill into something spectacular.

In the end, she chose the oven-baked breaded Brie with cranberry relish, followed by local cod served with a basil and parmesan risotto.

He raised an eyebrow at her choice. 'So you're a foodie, then.'

'Definitely. I'd rather enjoy my food than sit nibbling on a lettuce leaf, knowing that I'm fashionably stick-thin but being utterly miserable because I also know just how much I'm missing out on.'

Then she remembered some of the names she'd seen him linked with. Stick-thin model types, the lot of them. 'Sorry. I wasn't commenting on your…um…taste in female company.'

He laughed. 'I know. But I also know what you mean. It's easier to enjoy a meal with someone who's interested in what they're eating rather than someone who orders a starter for their main course and refuses pudding and you know they're counting calories and carbs the whole time.' He'd chosen grilled tiger prawns with lemon, followed by a plain steak, salad and new potatoes.

'Going for the manly option?' she teased.

'No. I just like my food simple and good quality.'

'How about pudding?' Although he'd skipped pudding at the pizza place, Sara knew he had a weakness for posh chocolate biscuits. The chances were, he'd also enjoy chocolate pudding.

'I'm not that bothered, but choose what you like.'

'The one I'd like is a sharing pudding—the fruit platter with white chocolate dip. But it's a bit too much for one.'

'Fine. I'll share it with you. Now, wine—you're having fish, so we'll go for white. Chablis OK with you?'

'Lovely—but you're having steak.'

'Which can cope perfectly well with good white wine. It doesn't have to be red,' he said. 'I suppose we could have champagne, but personally I think it's overrated. I'd rather have a decent Chablis—a Margaux or a Nuit St Georges.'

She smiled at him. 'And there's you teasing me about being posh.'

'You're saying a barrow boy can't enjoy wine?' he fenced.

She laughed. 'I'm not a wine snob—Justin is, but I guess that goes with the territory of being a barrister. I just know what I like.'

'Which is?'

'Pretty much the same as you, actually.' Though her budget didn't usually run to drinking it in restaurants.

'If we eat at seven,' Luke said, 'we can watch the sun set. So I'll order from room service; then we can unpack and maybe have a cup of coffee on the balcony.'

It didn't take long to unpack. And sitting on the balcony, watching the sea swishing in and out, was incredibly relaxing. The perfect weekend break. And even Luke had lost that slightly watchful look she was used to. He'd rolled the sleeves of his shirt up slightly, exposing a sprinkling of dark hair on his arms, and he looked utterly edible.

Down, girl, she told her libido silently. Luke, despite his teasing in the boat, might not appreciate being pounced on. And he certainly hadn't made a move towards her; when her fingers had brushed against his earlier as she'd handed him a cup of coffee, there hadn't been even the tiniest flicker of awareness on his face. No spark, like the one that had coursed through her.

Or maybe he was just better than she was at masking his feelings.

She had no idea what was going on between them right now. Whether they were colleagues or lovers. Not friends, certainly: on the boat, she'd noticed his barriers going up. When she'd touched his hand, he hadn't relaxed and laced his fingers through hers. In fact, he'd looked distinctly uncomfortable.

Probably because, as he'd admitted, he didn't like children—and their trip had definitely been family-oriented. Someone, she thought, must have hurt him very badly. There hadn't been a mention of a wife and children in his past, but she knew better than to ask straight out. Though a messy divorce would explain why he was so against relationships, why he didn't believe in love.

Right at that moment, he was calm. Reposed. And she wasn't going to risk ruining the moment by asking him where she stood or pushing him to talk about his past.

A knock at the door heralded room service—a waitress who swiftly laid the table on the balcony with a damask tablecloth, shiny cutlery and sparkling glasses, followed by a waiter who brought the wine and their starters.

The food turned out to be as good as the service. 'This,' she said after the first mouthful of her Brie, 'is perfect. Try it.'

He gave her an amused look, but allowed her to feed him with a forkful. 'Agreed, it's good,' he said. 'Try this.'

There was something decidedly sensual about opening her lips and allowing him to slide a tiger prawn into her mouth, and her heart skipped a beat at the look in his eyes. 'It's good,' she said. And she didn't just mean the food.

The idea of sharing a platter of fruit and melted chocolate with him made pleasure slide all the way down her spine. Would he keep things strictly professional with her—or would he feed her morsels of fruit? Would it start out as pudding and end up as something else?

Their main courses were just as spectacular, and then the waitress brought the fruit platter. There was a pot of melted chocolate over a tea-light candle to keep it warm, and as well as the pineapple and strawberries and papaya there were bite-size squares of home-made Yorkshire parkin and tiny short-bread rounds.

Sara speared a square of the ginger cake and dipped it in the chocolate. She was just about to draw it up to her mouth when Luke leaned forward and nibbled it off her skewer.

'Hey! That was mine,' she protested.

He raised an eyebrow. 'It's a sharing platter, I think,' he said, 'this is how it's meant to work.' And then he dipped a square of parkin into the chocolate and lifted it to her mouth. 'Open wide,' he said, his voice slightly husky.

This was a game she liked. And she could tell by the way his pupils were expanding that he enjoyed it, too. The setting sun was forgotten; all she could concentrate on was Luke.

'There's chocolate on the corner of your mouth,' he said when they'd finished, then leaned over and licked it off.

She wasn't sure which of them moved first, but the next thing she knew she was sitting on his lap, his mouth was jammed against hers and her hands were in his hair.

'I think,' he murmured when he broke the kiss, 'we'd better go back inside. Or anyone looking up is going to get an eyeful of something they shouldn't.'

Oh, help. She'd been so involved in his kisses that she'd actually forgotten where they were.

'Just as well I said we'd leave the stuff outside our door when we've finished.' He stole another kiss. 'Because I really do *not* want to be disturbed for the rest of this evening.' He lifted her as he stood up, then strode with her into the bedroom and laid her back against the pillows. 'Wait for me. Two minutes,' he said, brushing his mouth against hers.

She heard the clatter of china and cutlery—clearly he was dealing with the remains of their meal—and a door closing, and then he was back in the bedroom. Closing the heavy curtains. Switching on the bedside light.

'Sara,' he said.

She stood up and walked into his arms. Matched him kiss for kiss, touch for touch.

'I need this, too,' she whispered.

'I'm all yours,' he said.

So she'd tamed the pirate king, had she? Somehow, she thought not. But she took pleasure in unbuttoning his shirt and pushing it off his shoulders, exploring his muscular chest and broad shoulders. Unwrapping a parcel was half the fun, and she was going to enjoy every single moment of taking Luke's clothes off. Looking and touching and tasting.

'A proper six-pack,' she said, letting her fingers drift down over his abdomen. 'So this is what kick-boxing does for you, is it?'

'And the training for it.'

'Good,' she said, and unbuttoned his trousers. Slid the zip down incredibly slowly, keeping her gaze fixed on his—and she revelled in the fact that his breath hissed as her fingers moved lower. His earlier coolness had been a sham. Luke Holloway was definitely interested.

'Lose the shoes,' she said.

'Bossing me about again, are you?' But he kicked them off. She smiled. 'And now…'

But as she was about to push the material of his trousers over his hips, his hands grasped her wrists. Firmly enough to stop her, yet gently enough not to hurt.

'My turn,' he said. 'Arms up.'

She let him tug the hem of her strappy top and pull it over her head.

Then he undid the button and zip of her trousers. She'd already kicked her shoes off much earlier, so when the linen fell to the floor she simply stepped out of them.

'Now there's a picture,' he said. 'I knew you'd be the type to wear matching underwear.'

'Did you, now?'

'Those teal suede stilettos you were wearing yesterday…I could imagine you wearing just them and your underwear—matching teal silk and lace—and that string of black pearls.'

'You've been fantasising about me in my underwear?' The idea sent a kick of desire through her.

'Yes. And a bit worse than that,' he admitted with a mischievous grin. 'Like taking it off.'

'Show me,' she invited, and colour slashed across his cheekbones.

Firstly, he loosened her hair so it fell about her shoulders. Then he slid the narrow straps of her bra down her arms. 'You have beautiful shoulders,' he whispered, nuzzling kisses along them. 'And your skin's so soft. It makes me want to taste you.' He nibbled gently at the curve of her neck, making her shiver and tip her head back.

'And it makes me want to do this.' He dipped a finger under the lacy hem and traced the edge of her bra; every nerve-end seemed to come to life under his touch. Then he unclipped her bra slowly, with one hand; as it dropped to the floor, he let her breasts spill into his hands. 'You're stunning, Sara.'

Given the kind of women he dated—women who were a little taller and a lot thinner—she wasn't convinced—but then he bent his head and kissed her shoulders again, tracing kisses along her collarbone and then nuzzling down between her breasts. When he dropped to his knees in front of her and took one nipple into his mouth, her knees buckled and she had to hold on to his shoulders for support.

'Hold that thought,' he said, and hooked his thumbs into the sides of her knickers. Slowly, teasingly slowly, he drew them down to her ankles, then lifted her foot to help her step out of them. Then he rocked back on his haunches and looked up at her. 'Sara Fleet, you blow my mind.'

It was pretty much mutual. Not that she wanted to tell him yet. She held her hands out; when he took them, she tugged him to his feet. 'My turn.'

And then she copied his actions, dropping to her knees in front of him. She finished unzipping his chinos and stroked the material down over his hips; when they slid to the floor, she helped him step out of them and removed his socks at the same time.

She could see his erection outlined by the soft material of

his jersey boxer shorts; giving him a wicked grin, she breathed teasingly along it, so he'd feel the heat of her mouth, and she was rewarded with a husky groan of pleasure.

She stroked his thighs, firm and muscular. 'You're beautiful, Luke Holloway. If I was any good at art I'd love to paint you. Sculpt you.'

'Sounds like an excuse to look at me naked.' His words were teasing but his voice was slightly shaky. Her touch obviously affected him more than he was prepared to admit.

'Now there's an idea,' she teased back. 'And, considering that you took my clothes off…' She removed his soft jersey boxer shorts.

'Enough,' he said, reaching down to take her hands and pulling her to her feet. 'Much more teasing and I'm going to lose control.'

'Which would be a bad thing?'

'Considering that I want to make sure it's good for you— yes,' he told her baldly.

He lowered his mouth to hers, then picked her up and, still kissing her, carried her to the bed and set her back against the soft, soft pillows. He opened a drawer in the cabinet next to the bed to retrieve his wallet and remove a condom from it. She closed her hand over his. 'Mine,' she said softly.

He gave her a smouldering glance and the sexiest grin she'd ever seen.

He lay back against the pillows and she opened the foil packet; she rolled the condom onto his erect penis, teasingly slowly, looking him straight in the eye as she did so.

'Hear that shredding sound?' he asked.

'No.'

'I can. It's my patience and my self-control. If you're going to do it, Sara… Just do it.'

'What happened to finesse?' she teased. But she loved the idea that she could turn this quick, clever man into a pile of mush. So she finished rolling on the condom, straddled him and slowly lowered herself onto him.

'Yes.' The word was a hiss of pleasure. He shifted slightly so he could push more deeply into her, and she began to move over him, varying the pace and the pressure. He'd reached back over his head to grip a rail on the wrought-iron bedstead, and his knuckles stood out white; his breathing was growing shallower and faster as his climax built.

This was power.

And she loved every second of it.

Loved the fact that she was taking him to the edge of pleasure.

Then he released his grip on the bedstead and twined his fingers through hers. 'Look at me, Sara,' he whispered. 'See what you do to me.'

She did. Exactly the same as he did to her. She could feel the ripples of pleasure starting to spread and overlap. And she could see in his face, the moment that his climax hit, dovetailing with hers. The moment when they both fell over the edge.

He wrapped his arms round her, drawing her down to him; Sara rested her cheek next to his, enjoying the way he held her close. She knew that Luke wasn't a man who let people close but, after this, no way could he possibly put the barriers back between them. They'd shared too much.

And after he'd dealt with the condom, he curled his body protectively round hers, wrapping an arm round her waist and holding her close to him. She laced her fingers through his and he brushed a kiss against her shoulder. 'Sleep well,' he said softly.

'You, too.' And tomorrow… They'd deal with that when it arrived.

CHAPTER NINE

THE next morning, Luke woke Sara with kisses. Soft, sweet kisses that made her feel warm inside—a warmth that turned to heat when he began exploring her body with his mouth and his hands, finding places that made her want to purr with pleasure.

'I have an idea,' he said.

'Mmm.' As long as he carried on doing exactly what he was doing, she'd say yes to almost anything.

'You need to put your hair up first.'

'Why?'

'Health and safety.'

How come his brain was still functioning, when hers was out to breakfast? she wondered. She sat up—and then she remembered he'd loosened her hair the previous day. So she had no idea where her hairpins were. 'Sorry, no can do. Unless you tell me what you did with my hairpins.'

He looked blank for a moment, then grinned. 'Ah, yes. Give me a second.' A quick hunt on the floor, and he'd retrieved most of them from among their discarded clothes.

She put her hair up and let him lead her to the bathroom.

So that was what he had in mind. Sharing a bath.

He switched on the taps. 'What you said yesterday about the spa bath—it made me think this might be nice.' He picked up the three little bottles on the side of the bath, sniffed each in turn, then added a couple of drops from one to the water.

Foam began to form on the surface, and Sara frowned. 'Hang on. If we're having a whirlpool bath—I thought you weren't supposed to use bubbles in one?'

'A couple of drops is fine, as long as it's low-foam and not oil-based. Too much, and we'll have to mop the floor.'

Well, of course he'd know. He owned spas and health clubs.

He helped her into the bath, then slipped into the water next to her. He turned off the taps and switched on the whirlpool, and immediately the tiny layer of froth was whipped into deep bubbles.

She'd once accused him of not having fun.

Ha. She hadn't had a clue. This man definitely knew about fun.

She pushed aside the thought that he'd probably done this quite a few times before. With quite a few different women. This was here and now. That was what they'd agreed, wasn't it?

He dabbed foam on the end of her nose, then laughed at her.

She retaliated, and a vigorous foam fight ensued. And then Luke pulled her onto his lap. 'It's a shame your hair has to stay up—because in this bath, with your hair down, you'd look like a mermaid. All alluring and sensual.'

She laughed. 'Hardly. Apart from the fact I have legs instead of a tail, my singing voice isn't great.'

'You'll have to dazzle my senses with a kiss instead, then.'

She did.

And he responded, to the point that they were almost too late for breakfast. Sara still felt guilty about the fact that their sheets were damp—Luke hadn't waited for either of them to dry themselves properly before he'd carried her back to bed—but he was completely unrepentant.

Despite the fact that they were the last ones in the restaurant, the waitress greeted them cheerily and brought them freshly squeezed orange juice along with really good coffee.

'It's Sunday, so I'm having a proper breakfast,' Luke said, and ordered soft creamy scrambled eggs, granary bread toast and crisp bacon.

The sea air—or maybe making love with Luke—had given Sara an appetite, so she joined him.

When they'd finished, she leaned back against her chair with a sigh of pleasure. 'That was an excellent choice on your part. Right now, I feel as if I could conquer the world.'

'I think your parents misnamed you. They should've called you Scary,' he teased.

She pulled a face at him and laughed. Right at that moment she felt eighteen again. And Luke, too, looked younger. More carefree.

It didn't take them long to pack and check out. 'I cheated you out of your paddle yesterday,' he said. 'So we'll do it today.'

'You really don't have to.' She'd pushed him into the seal trip and he'd hated that.

'No. You're right. It'd be fun. The sun's shining, it's summer and we're at the seaside.'

'Am I hearing things?' She blinked. 'Are you going to tell me next that you're not going to work today?'

He laughed. 'I'm not going *quite* that far.'

After he'd put their things in the car, they headed for the beach. To Sara's surprise and delight, at the edge of the beach Luke removed his shoes and socks, then rolled his black trousers up to his knees. With his white shirt partly undone and his sleeves rolled up, he looked just as she'd imagined him, all barefoot and sexy and gorgeous. And only the fact that they were in a public place stopped her grabbing him and kissing him stupid.

'Remember that film with Burt Lancaster in it?' she asked as they walked along the edge of the sea, the waves swirling round their ankles.

'Film?' He looked blankly at her.

'I forgot, you don't do TV or films. Anyway, there's this film from the 1950s called *From Here To Eternity*—a real classic. Deborah Kerr and Burt Lancaster kiss on this Hawaiian beach among the crashing waves. And…' Her mouth went dry.

She couldn't see his eyes behind his dark glasses, but she

was pretty sure she could guess at their expression because his voice had grown deeper, sexier. 'We could,' he said. 'But, apart from the fact that this is North Yorkshire, not Hawaii, and the sea's pretty calm today, I think we could end up getting arrested.' He drew the tip of his forefinger down her bare arm. 'Because we don't seem to be able to stop at kissing.'

Very true. They'd already proved it several times, to their mutual satisfaction. She moistened her lower lip, and he groaned.

'Don't. Because it makes me want to taste you.'

It was the same for her.

'I need a cold shower,' he said.

'I could push you into the sea.' Except then his chinos and his shirt would be plastered against his skin, reminding her of the lake scene in *Pride and Prejudice*—a moment she'd savoured on several occasions with friends and wine and chocolate. 'Uh. Scratch that. We need ice cream.'

'After the breakfast we've just eaten?'

'To cool down,' she said.

He didn't take her hand as they walked to the little kiosk. Which was just as well. She had a feeling that as soon as they touched they'd combust. She bought them both a whippy cornet with a chocolate flake, then wished she hadn't when she watched him eating his; the way his tongue curled round the ice cream reminded her of the feel of his mouth against her skin.

In retaliation, she sucked on the end of her chocolate flake, and was rewarded with a groan. 'I'm going to have to turn my back,' he said, 'because you've put all sorts of ideas in my head, and they're definitely not suitable for the middle of a public beach.'

'You started it.'

'How?'

'Licking that ice cream.'

There was an impish quirk to his mouth. 'It's how you're supposed to eat ice cream.'

'Even so. It was positively indecent.'

He laughed. 'And what you just did was demure, was it?'

In answer, she just licked her lips, and he groaned. 'You're a bad, bad girl. And I'm very glad you are.'

When they'd both dried off and put their shoes back on, Luke drove them back to London. Though it wasn't quite the same as their journey north—apart from the fact that there were no traffic jams, Luke didn't ask her to make calls or check his diary, and they stopped halfway for a late lunch in a little pub in a village off the motorway.

Back in London, Luke parked the car outside Sara's block of flats in Camden.

'I'll carry your suitcase up for you,' Luke said.

'Thanks. Do you want to come in for a coffee?' Sara asked.

At six in the evening, there was a fair chance that her brother Justin was home. Luke really wasn't in the mood for meeting any of Sara's family—but, then again, how bad could it be? Justin knew they'd gone away on business, so it wasn't as if he'd start playing the tough big brother, grilling his baby sister's new boyfriend about his intentions. Besides, Luke could see in Sara's eyes that she'd be disappointed if he said no. So he could do this. Treat it like a business meeting. 'Sure. Coffee would be lovely.'

She tapped in the code on the keypad by the front door, then led him up the stairs to the first floor and unlocked the door to the flat.

'Oh. Justin isn't home.'

'Pity,' he lied. 'Where do you want me to put your case?'

'Leave it here in the hallway. Come through,' she said, ushering him into the living room. 'I'll bring the coffee in.'

Sitting and waiting patiently wasn't Luke's thing, so instead he wandered round the living room. The mantelpiece was full of photographs, including graduation photographs; one was Sara, and the family likeness told him that the others were her two brothers and Louisa. There was another photograph with

Louisa wearing a wedding dress, Sara in a bridesmaid's dress and their brothers in top hats and tails, another that was obviously of their parents, and less formal ones of a toddler he assumed was Louisa's. There was a photograph of their father walking through an orchard with four assorted dogs, and one of their mother up to her arms in flour in a farmhouse kitchen, clearly spontaneous rather than posed—her smile, he thought, was very like Sara's.

A close-knit family.

A world away from his own—well, his was close, but only if you toed the family line. Which he hadn't wanted to do. Whereas Sara's family... He had a feeling they'd all encourage each other to follow their dreams, even if they weren't in line with the rest of the family. After all, Justin was a barrister and Sara was an office troubleshooter—neither of which had anything to do with their parents' orchard.

Unsettled, he joined Sara in the kitchen. 'Want a hand with anything?'

'No, you're fine.' She was reading a note and smiling; she looked up at him over the edge. 'Justin left me this in the middle of the table, so I couldn't miss it. He went home for lunch today. Mum says she missed me and she's sent me some apple cake.'

'Apple cake?'

'Kentish speciality. And obviously Mum's big on apple recipes because of the business.' She grinned. 'Justin's a star. He stopped off at a supermarket on the way home and restocked the freezer with my favourite ice cream.'

'You and your ice cream,' he teased.

'Absolutely. And I love this bit. "Hope you had a chance for your paddle and you didn't work all weekend."' She laughed.

It was all affectionate and warm—and it scared the hell out of Luke because it was so far from what he was used to. In the days when he had a family, they never used to do little things to please each other; everything had been focused around the family business and the strange code of honour among thieves. Looking back, he remembered that his mother had diamond earrings, but he could never remember his father bringing her flowers or a box of chocolates or some little thoughtful token. And any paintings he'd done at school had always been left on the side, never pinned up on the wall.

Sara finished making the coffee; she added sugar to his mug and milk to hers. 'So can I tempt you?'

'Tempt me?'

She rolled her eyes. 'Wake up. *Apples.* Would you like some Kentish apple cake?'

'No, thanks. I'm fine.'

'Your loss,' she said. 'My mum's cooking is the best. OK, so this is reheated, but even the smell of it reminds me of home. She cooks this in the Aga and the whole house smells of apple and cinnamon. It's gorgeous.' She took a covered box from the fridge and spooned some of the apple cake into a bowl. 'Do you mind if we sit out here?' she asked.

'No, it's fine.' And there were fewer photographs to unsettle him than there were in the living room. Just postcards attached to the fridge with little magnets.

He sat at the table, his hands wrapped round his mug of coffee, while she warmed up the apple cake. The scent of cinnamon made his mouth water.

'Sure you don't want a taste?' she asked as she retrieved the bowl and added ice cream.

He thought of the way they'd shared a pudding the previous night. And how easy it would be to do it all over again. And how embarrassed Sara would be if her brother came home while Luke was still naked in her bed. So it was best not to start anything. 'Sure.'

'Good. All the more for me.' She looked slightly put out. 'I didn't know Justin was going home today.'

'So I've kept you from your family.'

She shrugged. 'It doesn't matter. I'll go next weekend.'

'Go tomorrow,' he said. 'Remember, you have the next two days off in lieu for this weekend.'

She looked straight at him, her blue eyes just a little too bright for his liking. 'So now what? We go back to a formal office relationship?'

'Yes. No.' Oh, hell. Whatever he said, whatever he did, he was going to hurt her. He really shouldn't have been so self-indulgent. Why hadn't he kept her at a proper distance, the way he'd meant to? He dragged a hand through his hair. 'Sara, I don't do happy-ever-after. And I don't want to do the wrong thing by you.'

'But?'

'But right now I don't want it to end,' he admitted. 'And I'm never indecisive like this. I always know what I'm doing.' He sighed. 'This has thrown me. I didn't expect to…' His voice faded. Of course he hadn't fallen in love with Sara Fleet. Even if he believed in love—which he didn't—he knew it didn't happen that fast. It couldn't possibly happen that fast.

'So what do you suggest?' she asked softly.

'As we said yesterday. Take it day by day. See how it goes. No pressure. No promises.' He spread his hands. 'I'm sorry, Sara. I can't offer you more. I just…'

'You've been focused on your business. And you don't want any distractions.'

He was relieved that she understood. 'I know it sounds selfish.'

'Sounds?' She arched an eyebrow.

'*Is*, then. But it's all I can offer you right now.'

'I wasn't looking for a rel…' Her voice faded.

He took her hand. Kissed her palm. Folded her fingers round it. 'He hurt you that much?'

'Who?'

'The guy who's made you wary of relationships.'

'What makes you think there's a guy?'

He noticed that she didn't actually deny it—just answered a question with a question. 'Because you,' he said simply, 'aren't the closed-off sort.' Those photographs, all smiles and hugs, had told him exactly what sort of woman Sara was. Warm and sweet—and way too good for him. 'So someone must have hurt you to make you back away. And I'd guess that it was the person you told me "wasn't so nice".'

'I don't repeat my mistakes.'

'And you think I'll be a repeat mistake?' he asked.

She swallowed. 'You're a workaholic. Like Hugh was.'

'No. I'm a workaholic, I admit, but I'm not Hugh,' he corrected. 'I'm *me*. I don't claim to be perfect, but I won't hurt you intentionally.'

'Hmm.'

He sighed. 'Just remember that I'm a man, not a mind-reader. If you're not happy about something, I need you to tell me. Be straight with me. Remember, I'm used to being on my own.'

She coughed. 'More like, you're used to being with a string of women.'

'I've never dated more than one woman at a time,' he said. 'That's dishonourable. Not my style.'

She said nothing. So was that what had happened? Her ex had two-timed her? But even if he asked her straight, he had a feeling she wouldn't tell him. The guy must have hurt her really badly—and he was surprised to feel himself tensing up. Wanting to flatten him. Ridiculous. Especially when he knew that violence solved nothing.

He stroked her face with the backs of his fingers. 'If it's easier for you, we could play it safe and go back to being business associates.'

'But?'

Clearly she'd picked up his line of thought. 'But I'd always wonder if I should've been a bit braver and taken the risk. And I think you would, too.'

She looked serious. 'So you think it's worth a try?'

'Only one way to find out. Live a little,' he said softly.

He was about to kiss her goodbye—chastely—and leave,

hen he heard the sound of a key in the door. A couple of
econds later, the kitchen door opened and a man strode in—
learly Justin, because Luke recognised him from one of the
hotographs.

'Hello, Shrimp! Sorry I was out when you got back.' Justin
reeted his sister warmly with a hug, a kiss and a ruffle of her hair.

'I'll forgive you. You restocked on ice cream for me.' She
eamed at him.

'Well, I have to keep my little sister happy.'

'Absolutely, if you want me to cook for you. Justin, this is
uke. Luke, this is my ancient, elderly brother.'

'Nice to meet you, Luke.' Justin's handshake was firm, dry
nd professional, and Luke found himself relaxing slightly. 'I
ope Shrimp here remembered her manners and offered you
ome apple cake rather than scoffing the lot herself.'

'She did.'

'Good. So, how was Scarborough?'

'Crossed off my list. I would've seen it as a challenge but—'
uke looked over at Sara '—luckily I had someone with me
ith some common sense.'

'No doubt you paid for it in whippy ice creams,' Justin said
ith a grin. 'I'm surprised she hasn't managed to persuade Dad
open a dairy.'

'It's a brilliant idea. It'd complement the apples. Ice cream
nd apple cake are the perfect partners. And we could do apple
orbet,' Sara said. 'Expand that to elderflower, from the trees
t the edge of the orchard. And maybe—'

'Enough, enough!' Justin held up his hands in surrender,
ughing.

Luke found himself liking the man: he had the same warmth
nd sense of fun as Sara. And he ended up staying much longer
an he'd expected to. When he left and Justin shook his hand
nd said, 'Good to meet you', Luke was able to echo the senti-
ent and mean it.

Though he also shook hands with Sara, rather than kissing

her. He wasn't quite ready to go public on a relationship where neither of them was completely sure where they were going.

'See you Wednesday,' he said.

She smiled back. 'See you Wednesday,' she echoed.

CHAPTER TEN

THE next morning, Sara woke at her usual time. And although she tried turning over and going back to sleep—knowing that she was officially on a day off—she couldn't settle.

Eventually, she gave up and looked at the clock. Seven o'clock. It was pointless just lying there. She might as well get up, have breakfast…and go into the Docklands office.

When she walked in at nine o'clock sharp, Luke glanced up from his desk and stared at her, looking surprised. 'Hello. I thought you were on a day off?'

'I changed my mind,' she said simply.

'What about your theory about the twenty per cent productivity drop?' he asked.

She shrugged. 'You'll have to live with it.'

He smiled. 'Then sit down. I'll make us some coffee.'

'I've been thinking,' she said when he returned with the coffee. 'We need to set some ground rules.'

'Sounds like you've already worked some out.'

'I have.'

'And?'

'One—and this is *not* negotiable—you don't sleep with anyone else while you're with me.'

'Fine. And it goes both ways,' he added.

'Agreed. Two, we're taking this day by day.'

'Agreed.'

'Three…' She'd been thinking about this one. A lot. It wa where things had started to go wrong with Hugh. 'You spend time with me. You don't work ridiculous hours.'

'I don't work ridic—' He stopped, mid-protest. 'OK. I'l compromise—I won't work quite as late as I have in the past. He could always catch up early in the morning. 'But I should warn you I have some standing dates. Including Monday nights.

'Dates?'

'Yup. You know. Things that involve me getting hot and sweaty. With lots and lots of physical action.'

Her eyes narrowed. 'Indeed.'

He leaned back against his chair. 'But if you want to be re sponsible for Karim not having his weekly game of squash with me on Monday nights and getting really unfit and flabby, sure I'll cancel.'

The rat. He'd strung her along. Teased her. And she'd been gullible enough to fall for it. 'Squash.'

He spread his hands. 'I told you I play squash a couple o times a week. Monday's with Karim and Thursday's a leagu match. And kick-boxing's on Tuesday and sometimes Wednes day.' He paused. 'You can come and watch, if you want.'

He didn't sound too enthused about the idea, though. Sh could guess why. 'It'll cramp your style.'

'No. It'll just be incredibly boring for you.'

That wasn't the real issue, she was sure. 'You don't wan anyone to know about me, do you?'

'Sara, any man would be happy to boast that he was dating you The word hung in the air—she said it for him. 'But…?'

He sighed. 'If you come to the squash court, Karim will take one look at you, leap to conclusions and get Lily to nag m stupid. I'll never get another minute's peace. And, right now this is very new—for both of us. So I want to keep things jus between us until we're sure of where it's going.'

She couldn't argue with that.

'But I could meet you afterwards. I know an excellen

Chinese restaurant not far from the squash courts, if you don't mind eating a bit late. They make the best dim sum ever.'

He was trying to compromise, she could tell. And it wasn't as if she wanted to spend every single evening with him. 'I still want to see my friends, too.'

'Good. Because cutting yourself off from your social network to spend all your time with one person is incredibly unhealthy.'

Did that mean he still intended to go to all those flash parties? And, most probably, on his own?

It must have been obvious what she was thinking, because he smiled. 'Hey, I'm bored with the party circuit. I'd offer to take you, but I can assure you that you'd be bored to tears within minutes. And, anyway, men aren't like women. They don't need bonding sessions.'

'No? What about football and beer?'

'I'm not into spectator sport,' he reminded her. 'Sure, I have the occasional beer with Karim after squash, but men don't sit around dissecting emotional stuff the way women do.'

'That's a bit sweeping.'

'Largely true, though.' He wrinkled his nose. 'Anyway, there's another reason why you have to keep up with your female friends—because there's no way you're dragging me off to see some tedious chick-flick.'

'You never know, you might enjoy it.'

He shook his head. 'I might enjoy sitting in the back row with you and kissing you stupid...but then again, I'd rather kiss you in private, so I can take things to their proper conclusion.'

'Proper?' she teased.

He laughed. 'OK, so what I have in mind is improper. But possibly not at this time of the morning, when I have meetings to go to and work to do.'

'How long have you been here?' she asked.

'Not long.'

'Crack of dawn?'

'No. I had a workout first,' he admitted.

'In one of your gyms?' At his nod, she sighed. 'And I be
you managed to get a meeting in there, too.'

'A teensy, teensy one.' He held his thumb and forefinger a
couple of millimetres apart.

'There's no hope for you, is there?' she asked ruefully.

He grinned. 'No. But if you want to try any persuasion tech
niques, I'm open to suggestions.' He glanced at his watch
'Gotta go. See you later.'

For a second, she wondered if he was going to kiss he
goodbye. Then again, this was the office. And of course Luk
would be professional with her here. She damped down the dis
appointment, waited for her computer to boot up, and startec
working through the emails.

Two seconds later, the office door opened and Luke strode
back in. 'Forgot something,' he said.

'Uh-huh.' She could be just as professional as he was. She
carried on working, assuming that he was going over to his desk

And then he spun her chair round. Leaned over her. Anc
kissed her. Thoroughly.

'Later,' he said softly, and left the office.

And it took a good ten minutes before Sara was calm enoug
to concentrate on her work.

Luke was out of the office for most of the day, and Sara wa.
in the middle of emailing him to say she was leaving for th
day when he walked in.

'Hi there. Sorry, got held up,' he explained. 'Is everything
OK?'

'Fine.' She smiled at him.

'Is there anything I need to know about?'

'Apart from what I've already sent you? No. I was just abou
to go home.'

'Five o'clock on the dot?' he teased. 'You weren't suppose
to be here anyway. You could've left earlier, if you'd wanted
Gone shopping or something.'

'Shoe shopping?' she teased.

He took a look under the desk. 'Yet another different pair. Are you sure your name isn't really Imelda?'

'No, but Lou changed our spaniel's name to Imelda, because he steals shoes and piles them up in his bed. He never chews them—just cuddles them. And it's always one from everyone in the house.' She laughed. 'Lou says it's because he thinks it'll mean we can't go out without him.'

She noticed that Luke looked faintly awkward. Because he wasn't a dog person? Or was it the fact that she was talking about her family? Despite telling her about his dad teaching him to fly the kite, Luke never said a word about his family, so it was a fair bet they weren't close.

'Are you still OK to eat with me tonight?' he asked.

'Sure.'

'Good.' He took the notepad from her desk and scribbled down an address. 'This is the restaurant. Meet you there at eight?'

'Fine.' So he planned to meet her there rather than outside the squash courts. He really did like to keep his life compartmentalised, she thought.

He opened his wallet and took out a couple of notes, proffering them to her. 'Take a taxi.'

She folded her arms. 'I'm perfectly capable of getting the Tube.'

He sighed. 'You're female, you're on your own and it's the evening.'

'It's still light at eight o'clock,' she pointed out.

'I don't care.' He put the notes on the desk in front of her. 'Take a taxi there, and I'll see you home.'

'Has feminism completely passed you by?' she asked.

'No,' he said. 'I believe in equal opportunities. But I also believe in not taking stupid risks to make a point. It's not a particularly rough area, and I know you're streetwise—but you also don't know the area, which makes you vulnerable. So stop being stubborn about it and take a taxi. And wait inside the restaurant for me. I'll book a table in my name.' He folded his arm and stared at her.

Sara knew when she was beaten. 'All right. Thank you. Even though I think it's completely unnecessary and over the top.' She tucked the notes into her purse, then switched off he computer. 'See you at eight. Have a good match.'

'Thanks.' He smiled at her and headed for his own desk a she left the office.

He was going through his emails when she returned.

'What?' he asked.

'As the saying goes…"I forgot something."' She spun hi chair round, the way he had to her that morning, bent her hea and kissed him, deepening the kiss and exploring his mouth.

By the time she broke the kiss, his pupils were enormous there was a slash of colour across his cheeks and his mouth wa slightly swollen and reddened.

'How the hell am I supposed to concentrate after that? he demanded.

'You're the genius. I'm sure you'll work something out.' Sh gave him a cheeky grin and sashayed out of the office, knowing that he was watching every move she made.

At five to eight that evening, she was waiting in the restau rant; true to his word, Luke had booked them a table. She sa facing the door so he'd see her as soon as he walked in, ordered a mineral water and was browsing through the menu whe something made her look up.

Luke.

Funny that her senses were so attuned to him, she knew the second he'd walked in the door. It had never been lik that for her before. Not even with Hugh—and she'd been s sure that she and Hugh would marry and settle down an have children.

With Luke, she wasn't sure of anything. They were takin this day by day, and he'd been up front about the fact he dislike children. Quite what the future held for them, she didn't know

But, for the life of her, she couldn't just walk away without seeing where this took them.

'I'm so glad you don't believe in making a man wait for you to make a dramatic entrance,' Luke said, brushing his mouth against hers and sliding into the seat opposite hers.

His hair was still damp from the shower, and he looked utterly gorgeous in plain black trousers and a black cashmere sweater. He'd drawn admiring glances from several tables on his way over to her; it wasn't just the way he looked, but the way he moved. All loose-limbed and sexy.

And all *hers*.

'How was your squash match?' she asked.

'Someone completely destroyed my concentration earlier,' he said. 'So what do you think?'

She batted her eyelashes. 'Are you saying you lost because of little ol' me?'

'Yup. So the very least you can do is kiss me better.'

'In the middle of a restaurant?' She wagged her finger at him. 'Tut, tut, Mr Holloway. You need to learn some patience.'

'You're trying mine right now.'

She just laughed. 'I'm hungry.'

'So,' he said, 'am I.'

'Then let's order.'

He sighed. 'You really don't take a hint, do you?'

'You promised me food. And I thought you hotshot businessmen made a point of under-promising and over-delivering?'

'Yeah.' He laughed. 'You know, that dress looks fabulous.'

It was a red linen shift dress, teamed with a black lacy shrug and her black pearls. One of her favourites.

'Thank you. This all looks fabulous. What do you recommend?'

'Dim sum to start, then crispy duck. Then maybe share a mixture of dishes.'

It was the perfect evening. Good food, good company, good conversation.

And he held her hand all the way home on the Tube. He even came in for a coffee and chatted to Justin about cars and sound systems. To the point where Sara let herself begin to hope that this was going to work out. True, he didn't sit anywhere near her and he gave Justin the impression that dinner had been business rather than personal, but at least he stayed and talked.

'I'll see you tomorrow,' she said when she finally saw him to the door.

'No. You were supposed to take today off, and tomorrow you're definitely not in the office. Go and buy some shoes or something.'

'You're a bad influence,' she said with a smile. 'I never need encouraging to buy shoes.'

'Show them to me on Wednesday,' he said with a grin.

So he wasn't planning to see her tomorrow at all. OK. Well, this was new for both of them, and taking it slowly would be sensible. 'Mmm. And it'd be nice to have new shoes for tomorrow night—my regular pizza night with the girls.' Just so he'd know she wasn't pining over him. 'They, at least, will appreciate them.'

'And you're saying I won't?'

'You're a man,' she said loftily. 'Of course you won't. I'll see you Wednesday, then.' She reached up to kiss his cheek.

In response, he drew her closer. Kissed her mouth. Not with the hunger he'd kissed her that morning: this was a sweet, soft kiss of promise. The kind of kiss that made her feel as if her bones had just melted. The kind of kiss that stole her heart. 'Sweet dreams, Sara,' he said, and waited until she'd closed the front door behind her before walking away.

When Luke got home, he really intended to work. There were some reports on potential properties that he wanted to compare and contrast. But he couldn't concentrate the way he usually did. Every report he looked through, he found himself staring at the pictures of the hotel rooms and thinking of Sara and wondering how soft the bed was.

And it drove him crazy.

He never, but never, had a problem compartmentalising his work and his love life.

Or maybe it was because she worked with him. It couldn't be anything else, he was sure.

But he missed her the next day. Missed the sassy comments mingled with sound common sense and good ideas. Missed bouncing ideas off her. Missed her ready smile.

And the kick-boxing turned out to be even more of a disaster area than his squash match.

'Either you're working too hard or she's utterly gorgeous,' Mike, his sparring partner, said afterwards.

'Working too hard,' Luke fibbed. He knew exactly what the problem was. Sara. He couldn't stop thinking about her. And, against his better judgement, he ended up texting her later that evening.

Hope you're having a good evening. L.

It was completely innocuous, in case one of her friends picked up her phone by mistake. But enough to let her know he was thinking of her.

The reply came an hour later. *I am. Very girly. You'd HATE it.*

He almost—almost—suggested that she came over to his place for coffee afterwards. But that would be too needy, and he wasn't needy. Ever.

He left it half an hour before enquiring casually, *You busy tomorrow night?*

Why?

Have dinner with me?

The gap before she replied felt incredibly long, and Luke was cross with himself. Ridiculous. Sara wasn't a game player; she was probably on the Tube and didn't have a signal.

And then his phone beeped. *Thought you had kick-boxing on Weds?*

Skipping it. His concentration was so shot this week, he knew it was pointless. *So, dinner?*

What time?

After work. He suppressed the thought that tomorrow night he might get to find out whether her underwear co-ordinated with her shoes and her tops. *Any food you don't like?*

This time, instead of beeping to signal the arrival of a text message, his phone rang.

'Rather than playing text ping-pong, isn't it easier to have a conversation on the phone?' Sara asked crisply.

'You were out for the evening. I thought it was easier to send a text so you could answer at your leisure.'

'Well, I'm home now, so you can talk to me.'

He laughed. 'Now that's a dangerous invitation.'

'Why?'

He couldn't resist teasing her. 'What would you do if I gave you a dirty phone call?'

She laughed back. 'Probably enjoy it.'

He was speechless. She'd really called his bluff; right at that moment, he felt as if his tongue had been glued to the roof of his mouth.

'What did you have in mind for tomorrow night?'

You, me and nothing in between. He just about stopped himself saying it. 'Just dinner. Is there any food you don't like?'

'I'm easy to please. What's the dress code?'

'Whatever you like. Oh, and your new shoes.'

'I didn't buy any.'

'Oh.'

'But I did buy something else.' Her voice was full of amusement. And there was a sensual note that made him feel as if she were stroking his skin. Kissing her way down his body.

Uh.

He really, really had to get himself back under control. Before he said something really stupid. Like begging her to come over and show him this very second. And he really, really didn't want her to know just how needy he was feeling right now.

He didn't do needy. He'd spent half his life standing on his own two feet, and it was going to stay that way.

'Aren't you going to ask me what?' she teased.

'No. I'll see you tomorrow,' he said, more abruptly than he'd intended. 'Goodnight.' But when he cut the connection he felt awful.

What was wrong with him?

He *liked* Sara, for pity's sake. He enjoyed her company. So why was he blowing hot and cold like this, behaving like a moody teenager whose hormones were running riot?

There was an explanation—but it wasn't one he was prepared to countenance. How could you fall in love with someone when you didn't believe in love?

Utterly ridiculous.

So instead he went down to the office and worked through various sets of figures until he was too tired to see straight.

CHAPTER ELEVEN

'WHY didn't you tell me?' Sara asked as Luke unlocked his front door the following evening.

'What?'

'That you live above your office.'

He shrugged. 'It wasn't relevant.'

'Wasn't relevant?' She stared at him. 'Luke Holloway, I can't believe you sometimes.'

'What's the problem?'

'You work crazy hours *and* you live right above your office.'

He sighed. 'All it means is that I have a short commute to work. And I do leave my work in my office. I never bring work home with me.'

'You don't need to, do you? All you have to do is walk downstairs.' She shook her head. 'There's no hope for you.'

'Sara, I don't see what the fuss is about.'

'No. You wouldn't.' And it wasn't Luke's fault that her ex was out of the same mould. She shouldn't take out her insecurities on him. 'Sorry,' she muttered.

'Women. They're another species,' he said lightly. 'Come and see the views.' He ushered her into the living room. 'What do you think?'

It was as stunning as she'd guessed it would be, the very first day she'd seen the building. Luke lived in the duplex penthouse apartment, and his living room was right at the top of the tower. The side overlooking the Thames and the city was floor-to-ceiling glass, so the view was incredible. And, with the sun still out, the river sparkled—it was like looking down onto a magical world.

'It's fabulous,' she breathed.

'And that wall means the room gets lots of natural light. It's one of the things I love most about living here.'

In most other male preserves, she thought, there would be a state-of-the-art TV and several games consoles as the focal point of the room. But Luke's living room was furnished extremely simply. No clutter anywhere. Just three enormous leather sofas, which looked as if they'd be butter-soft to the touch, grouped round an extremely modern fireplace; a coffee table near one of the sofas; a stereo system which looked sleek and stylish and she'd just bet was the very top of the range; and a bookcase which seemed to contain mainly business-oriented textbooks. There was also a glass-topped dining table with eight chairs on the other side of the room. At one end of the table, two places had been set opposite each other with what looked like granite place mats, cutlery that shone with the lustre of real silver and the finest, thinnest crystal glasses. A fat white candle stood in a scooped silver bowl, nestled on top of flowing curved legs: a Celtic knot design, she thought, stripped down to its simplest form.

There wasn't a single photograph: nothing at all personal to give away what kind of man Luke was. They could've been standing in an extremely posh hotel suite. Admittedly, with that incredible glass wall, Luke didn't really need any pictures: the views were enough. Over the mantelpiece—bare of anything except a small unadorned clock—there was a large mirror, reflecting the views. And it made it very clear to her that Luke was completely self-contained. He didn't need anything or anyone.

This really didn't bode well for the beginning of their relationship, she thought.

Yet there had been moments in Scarborough where he'd

seemed to let her in. When he'd told her about his father teaching him to fly a kite, when he'd walked with her at the edge of the sea, when he'd shared the chocolate dipping platter with her. Or was she deluding herself?

'It's gorgeous—though it's pretty minimalist,' she remarked.

He shrugged. 'I hate clutter.'

She knew that already, from his office. He really wouldn't be able to cope with Louisa's toddler, Maisie, she thought—the little girl was going through the stage of trailing clutter everywhere.

'Would you like a glass of wine before dinner?' he asked.

'Thank you.' She followed him through to the next room; the kitchen had granite worktops, what looked like handmade pale wood cabinets and a state-of-the-art range cooker. There was practically nothing on any of the work surfaces, apart from a wooden fruit bowl and a kettle. No cork pin-board on the wall above the breakfast bar, crowded with memos and recipes and business cards, as there was in her parents' kitchen; no post-cards or photographs held onto the stainless steel American fridge with little magnets.

And, more to the point, she couldn't smell anything. Nothing cooking, nothing marinating.

Odd.

He took a bottle of Chablis from the fridge and poured them both a glass. 'Cheers,' he said, raising his glass in a toast.

'Cheers.' She paused. 'So if we're having dinner here tonight—does this mean you're cooking for me?'

'Not exactly.'

'I'm not with you…' Then the penny dropped and she grinned. 'Ah. You cheated and bought stuff you're going to heat up in the microwave.'

'Slightly worse,' he said.

'How much worse?'

'I sweet-talked the café manager at one of the gyms to make something for me that I could heat through,' he admitted. 'It's in the fridge.'

Unbelievable. 'You have a kitchen like this and you don't cook?' she asked, flabbergasted.

'I don't need to cook, apart from breakfast—and even then I might nip down to the coffee bar and grab a bagel because it's quicker. If I'm in the office, I'll have a sandwich for lunch.'

And eat it at his desk, with his other hand annotating reports, she thought. Apart from the occasion when she'd taken him to St Dunstan's and the time they'd gone to the pizza place. Lunch dates they hadn't repeated.

'Though if I'm at one of the businesses, I'll eat in the café there.'

'And you do the same for dinner.'

'Pretty much. I eat sensibly.' He shrugged. 'It's better than living on burgers and doughnuts. And it also means I get to do some quality checking on the health club cafés; I can make sure the food and the service are what I'd want them to be. Double whammy, you might say.'

She shook her head. 'You're missing out on a lot, you know. Cooking's one of the best ways I know to relax.'

His eyes lit with amusement. 'I know other ways. Though, if I give you a demonstration, dinner will be very, very late.'

She could guess exactly what he was talking about. And the remembered feel of his hands and his mouth against her skin sent a shaft of pure desire through her. To cover her confusion, she took a sip of wine and pretended he hadn't said a thing. 'I used to love cooking with my mum—mind you, I drove her insane because I was always rearranging her cupboards.' She smiled. 'Mum used to rearrange them right back and leave me sarcastic little notes for the next time I sneaked into the kitchen to do it.'

'Then you've always been the orderly type?' At her nod, he raised an eyebrow. 'So why were you giving me a hard time just now for having a tidy flat?'

'There's tidy, like me, and there's extreme minimalist,' she said.

'I get it. You like having all the clutter—but you also like having it all lined up and put away.'

'Yup.'

'I would really like to know,' he said, 'just how many pairs of shoes you have. And whether you arrange them by colour, style or fabric.'

'That,' she retorted, 'would be telling.'

'Come and sit down and I'll feed you,' he said. He held the chair out for her that faced the view.

'But that means you can't see the view,' she protested.

'I see it all the time.'

He was being polite, and she was the guest. She'd better remember that.

He lit the candle and the scent of vanilla filled the air.

'This is lovely—and I like that holder. The legs look a bit like a Celtic knot, only simpler.'

He smiled. 'What do you expect from—I quote—"an extreme minimalist"?' He walked over to the stereo system and pressed a couple of switches.

Sara raised an eyebrow as the first notes slid into the air. 'What, no dinosaur rock?' she teased.

'Hey, you're the one who had piano lessons as a kid. I assumed you'd like this.'

'You can never go wrong with Mozart,' she said. Good food accompanied by candlelight and the most beautiful piano music. Utter bliss. 'This sonata's one of my favourites.'

'Don't tell me—you can play it?'

'I used to be able to,' she admitted. 'But I haven't played for ages. I'd make a real mess of it now.'

'Would you rather I changed the music?' he asked.

'No, this is fine. Do you want a hand in the kitchen with anything?'

'No, that's OK. It's practically all done.'

He brought through two plates of prawns mixed with avocado and baby spinach leaves, drizzled with lime juice and olive oil.

'Wow, this is fantastic,' Sara said after the first taste.

'Exactly. So when I have food like this available, why would I bother cooking?'

'Point taken.'

The main course was cold chicken with baby new potatoes and salad. 'Are you telling me you actually sullied a saucepan with this?' she teased.

'You must be joking. Too much washing up,' he retorted.

'I love the dressing.'

'Pomegranate and orange. Apparently Cathy got the recipe for this one from Lily after we did a tasting thing for her.'

And pudding was utterly perfect. Fresh raspberries and best-quality vanilla ice cream. Had he remembered her favourite? she wondered.

'This,' she said, 'is bliss. My brothers and sister tease me about it, but you just can't get better than really good vanilla ice cream. Especially with lovely tart English raspberries.' She smiled. 'It always makes me think of the summer holidays when I was a kid, raiding the garden. There's nothing like fruit that's freshly picked and still warm from the sun when you eat it.'

'Glad you like it.'

'Well, that was fabulous. Even if it was utterly cheating on your part.'

'Hey, I washed the raspberries myself,' he protested, laughing.

'That,' she said, 'isn't cooking.'

'Yeah, yeah.' He cleared the table. 'Go and sit down in comfort. I'll bring the coffee through.'

Sara curled up on one of the huge leather sofas and just looked at the lights. Now it was dusk, the lights had come on outside, brilliant whites and deep blues reflected on the Thames. 'This is beautiful,' she said as Luke returned bearing coffee and a box of chocolates.

'Wait a second.' He went over to the table and blew out the candle. 'How about now?'

That little extra bit of darkness inside made the outside seem even brighter. 'Just stunning,' she said. She could understand exactly why he'd chosen to live here.

'It's even better late at night,' he said. 'The Thames is like polished ebony reflecting it all back.'

'Like a Whistler painting.'

He smiled. 'Trust you to know the art.'

'Don't be chippy.'

'I'm not. I don't know a huge amount about art, though I'm not that keen on abstract stuff. I like a painting to look like what it is.' He settled next to her, sharing the chocolates.

For a second, Sara could imagine every evening being like this. Living with Luke, sharing his space—cooking with him, laughing with him, making love with him.

Then she shook herself. She wasn't supposed to be letting herself fall for him. This was supposed to be getting the attraction out of their mutual systems.

Luke took her hand. 'So you like my living room. Want to come and see what I go to sleep to?'

Which didn't necessarily mean he was planning to make love with her, Sara reminded herself; he might be just offering her a guided tour of the rest of the flat. 'Sure,' she said, hoping that her voice didn't sound quite as breathless as it felt.

He led her downstairs. Although he didn't switch on the light in his bedroom, the glow from outside was enough to show her the contents: a huge, huge platform bed with plenty of pillows, a bedside table with a lamp and lots of space. As with the living room, one wall of the room was floor-to-ceiling glass; the bed was positioned to face the glass and, instead of curtains, he had narrow black Venetian blinds. Again, there were no pictures on the rest of the walls, and all the furnishings seemed to be in shades of grey and white.

Then she realised that the Mozart was still playing—and she could still hear it. 'How do you do that?'

'It's probably what you'd term boys and their toys.' He

gave her a wry smile. 'It's a sound system that follows you round the flat.'

'If you'd told me about it before I heard it for myself, I would've said you'd been reading too many sci-fi novels.' She shook her head in wonder. 'I had no idea that kind of technology even existed.'

'It's based on wireless networks,' he explained.

'It's impressive.' And she'd just bet it was hideously expensive. Especially given how good the quality of the sound was.

He inclined his head. 'Thank you.'

She wandered over to the window and looked out. 'This is astonishing.'

'I like it. And with all the glass…it makes me feel free.'

'You're claustrophobic?' she guessed.

'I couldn't have worked in the market if I was, with all the stalls right up together and everything piled high—no, I just like my space.'

Was that a warning, a reminder that he wasn't going to let her any closer? But, then again, he'd invited her here, shown her round the place.

She stood with her hands on the rail of the window, looking out and drinking in the view. Luke stood behind her and slid his arms round her waist. He brushed his mouth against the nape of her neck. 'I really can't work out whether I like your hair up or down best. Up means I get access like this…' He drew a trail of nibbling kisses along the sensitive curve at the side of her neck. 'And down makes you look much more touchable, less remote.'

'You think I'm remote?'

'When you're all elegant and sophisticated… Yes. And I'm glad today you wore a dress rather than a suit.'

'Why?'

'Because—' his fingers found the tab of her zip and lowered it '—it makes things easy for me.'

He was planning to undress her in front of a window? 'Luke, we can't—people might see!'

'Stop worrying,' he said. 'Apart from the fact we're on next to the top floor, there's no light on inside—the light's coming in from outside, so we can see out but people can't see in.'

'But, Luke…'

'It's fine,' he reassured her. 'Live a little.'

He kissed all the way down her spine until she was shivering, then he eased the material of her dress over her shoulders, drawing it slowly down to her waist and letting it fall to the floor.

She turned to face him. 'Luke.'

'I want to touch you, Sara.'

'And I want to touch you.' She unbuttoned his shirt. She could see his face clearly in the light spilling in through the window; his eyes were really dark, there was a slight hint of stubble on his jaw and, with that white shirt undone, he looked as sexy as hell.

He sucked in a breath. 'Do you have any idea how sexy you look right now? In lacy knickers, high heels and pearls, with your hair up?'

'This was what I bought yesterday. Well, except the shoes and necklace.' The pearls were palest lavender, matched to her underwear. 'You like them?'

'More than like.' He picked her up, carried her to his bed and settled her against the pillows while he ripped the rest of his clothes off.

The mattress was firm and the pillows were the kind you could sink into but which also gave support. His sheets were purest cotton with a really high thread count, so soft against her skin, and they were perfectly smooth, not even creased from being folded.

'What are you thinking?' he asked softly.

'Scarborough. The sheets weren't creased there, either.' Not until they'd spent the night in them.

'You can crease my sheets any time you like,' he teased. Then his face went serious and he kissed her, demanding a response from her mouth while he finished removing her clothes.

He paused to protect her with a condom, then eased into her body. And it felt to Sara as if she was really connecting with him—more than just bodily. He lost himself in her, just as she lost herself in him.

Afterwards, he took off her pearls and placed them on his bedside table before taking her through to his en-suite bathroom. His shower was definitely big enough for two, and he paid attention to every centimetre of her skin, lathering it and then rinsing off the suds. The towels were thick and fluffy, and he dried her very tenderly, really cosseting her.

And then amusement lit his eyes.

'What?' she asked.

'You're the only woman I've ever met who matches her toenail polish to her underwear.'

'Details are important,' she said. 'Actually, if my shoes aren't black, I normally match it to my shoes.'

'So you have dozens of bottles of nail polish as well as dozens of pairs of shoes?'

'Could be worse. I only have three handbags,' she teased back.

'We'd better get dressed,' he said. 'I'll drive you home.'

So he wasn't going to ask her to stay. Well, she hadn't expected it. Besides, she didn't have clean clothes and a toothbrush with her, so it was just as well. The fact that Luke had shared as much of himself with her as he had tonight was a huge step forward.

Luke came up to the flat with her. Justin was out for the evening and had left her a note but, to her disappointment, Luke didn't stay.

It must've shown on her face because he said softly, 'If I come in for coffee, you know as well as I do that it won't stop there. And I don't want to embarrass you in front of your brother.'

'Uh-huh.' She tried her best to sound cool and casual and perfectly OK with it all.

And then he kissed her goodnight; it was so sweet and tender and full of promise that it made her want to cry.

'See you tomorrow,' he said.

'Tomorrow.'

One day at a time, they'd agreed. If she pushed him too far, too fast, it would all blow up in her face. She just needed to be patient.

And then it hit her.

She'd fallen in love with Luke Holloway. A workaholic who didn't believe in marriage, who didn't want children and who, despite the fact that he'd been fine with her brother, would no doubt take the long way round to avoid anything resembling a family gathering. A man who didn't believe in happy-ever-afters.

The worst possible man she could fall for.

What made it even worse was that she knew he was definitely the one. Her feelings for Hugh paled into insignificance against what she felt for this man. This went bone deep.

She knew that Luke was going to need patience and time to trust her, to talk to her about whatever was in his head; he was a man who was totally self-contained. But would he ever really open up to her?

All the way back to Docklands, Luke thought about it. New territory. He'd always been careful to avoid his previous girlfriends' families. The fact that he'd met Sara's brother—and liked him—meant that he was getting in too deep for comfort.

He couldn't pull back. Not now. Yet the idea of going forward made him nervous. Crazy. He'd done deals for enormous amounts of money. Taken plenty of risks—calculated, but still risks. Yet he'd never felt upside down and in a whirl, the way he did whenever he thought about Sara.

If this was love, he wasn't sure he could cope with it. He wanted his nice, orderly, *busy* life back.

Though, at the same time, he couldn't imagine life without Sara around. He no longer wanted the shallow, glittering parties that had been his social life. No longer wanted a string of gorgeous women who expected no commitments, just lavish gifts and lots of fun.

What he wanted was something much simpler.

And much more complex.

He wanted Sara.

But if he took the risk—what then? Would he end up hurting them both? Would he end up losing her?

Because if he let her into his heart, took the risk and let her draw him into her family, he wasn't sure that he'd survive losing all that a second time.

There had to be a way forward. But, right at that moment, he couldn't see it.

CHAPTER TWELVE

OVER the next couple of weeks, Sara and Luke saw more of each other outside work, and she found herself beginning to hope that things might just work out for them. Luke delighted her one Saturday with a trip to a couple of ruined abbeys in Kent, saying, 'Seeing as I've taken up the time you were going to spend wandering round temples in Greece and Italy, this is the least I can do.' A day spent walking hand in hand, with lunch at a little country pub, quiet and intimate and close. Just perfect.

She, in turn, surprised him with tickets for a rock concert; although it wasn't really her thing, she could see how much he enjoyed it and that made it all worthwhile.

And, although Luke still hadn't found a temp, Sara didn't mind that much; she was enjoying working with him and liked the way he asked her opinions of things and stretched her skills by teaching her to read balance sheets and underlying trends. Even better was when he asked her to go with him to scope out potential hotels.

'Can you come with me to look at a place?' he asked.

'Oh, you mean that place you found in Cromer?' She remembered him talking about it: a seaside resort in Norfolk with a Victorian heyday. It was too late in the year to see the poppies the area had once been famed for, but it still held the potential of a paddle in the sea and a walk on the beach in the early evening, just before the light faded. 'Sure.'

'It's another weekend, I'm afraid—is that OK?'

She nodded. 'When?'

'Friday morning. I'll need you to meet me here at eight.'

Norfolk was only a couple of hours' drive away. Maybe, she thought, this wasn't the hotel he'd been talking about; maybe this was a new opportunity and he wanted to get the earliest look possible. 'I'll check my diary,' she said, wanting to make the point that she did have a life outside work and wasn't going to drop everything for him. 'Yes, you're OK. Though, had it been next weekend, I would've had to say no.' Not that it was worth asking Luke to come with her to her niece's birthday party. If he was reluctant to meet her oldest brother, no way would he agree to come to Kent for a Sunday afternoon and meet her entire family.

'Good. You'll need casual clothes. Flat shoes with a decent grip are a good idea.'

She frowned. 'I thought Norfolk was flat?'

'Obviously it's not mountainous like the Lake District but, apart from the fens and bits around Yarmouth, it's not that flat.'

'Flat shoes.' She surveyed the lipstick-red stilettos she was wearing. Definitely not suitable.

He laughed. 'Sounds like it's a chance for you to go shoe shopping. Oh, and your passport.'

'Passport? Why do I need that?'

'Because I need a photocopy of it—and your driving licence—for the insurance company. You know, to insure my car for you to drive.'

'Since when do they ask for a passport?'

He shrugged. 'Maybe they want extra proof of identity.'

Maybe companies were tightening up security.

'Oh, and don't bother with breakfast. We'll stop on the way.'

But on Friday morning he didn't drive her to Norfolk. Instead, they took the Docklands Light Railway to London City Airport.

'Luke? Where are we…?'

'You'll see when we get there' was the irritating reply.

'I thought we were checking out one of your potential hotels?'

'Nope. We're playing hooky for the weekend.'

She stared at him in surprise. 'But you don't play hooky.'

He smiled. 'Maybe you've inspired me.'

Maybe, she thought; she'd certainly noticed that he'd worked fewer hours recently.

Once they'd checked in, he bought them coffee and muffins

She laughed. 'So Mr Healthy does eat cake sometimes, then.'

He laughed back. 'Sometimes. And you know my weaknesses. Posh chocolate biscuits.' His eyes added the rest of it for him, and desire rippled down her spine.

The airport operated a silent terminal system; rather than a tannoy announcing the flights, there were information screens throughout the airport giving updates on arrivals and departures. There were several flights due, but Sara knew there was no point in asking him which one.

And then she saw it on the screen.

Private charter. Holloway.

'Private charter?' she asked. 'You chartered a plane just for us?'

'Don't get too excited. It's not a jumbo jet,' he said dryly. 'I know air travel isn't eco-friendly, but the rest of the trip is.'

'But…can you do that sort of thing? Charter a plane, just like that?'

'You can if you have a friend who owns an airline.'

She blinked. 'You have a friend who owns an airline?'

'A small one. We were on the same MBA course.'

She wasn't surprised that Luke had done an MBA. And she'd just bet that he'd graduated at the top of his class.

The plane was tiny—only six seats plus the pilot—but it meant she could see everything.

Four hours later, they landed at a tiny airport. 'Where are we?' she asked.

'Samos. Greece,' he added, for good measure.

Once they'd disembarked and gone through Customs, they

took a taxi to the harbour. 'Stay there a minute,' he said, and disappeared. When he returned, he picked up their cases and led her further down the marina to where a yacht was moored, its white sails unfurled.

She blinked. 'We're going on that?'

'Yup. You and me.'

'But I've never done any proper sailing.'

He looked amused. 'You don't need to.'

'You've hired a skipper?'

He smiled. 'This isn't a complicated boat, Sara. It only takes one to sail it—and, anyway, I can teach you rigging and steering, if you like.'

'You're kidding.' And he was going to sail the boat himself?

His grin broadened. 'What, you're chickening out on me? If I remember rightly, you were the one who was so keen on boats at Scarborough.'

'A boat trip,' she corrected, 'where I was a passenger and all I had to do was look at the seals.'

'You're still a passenger,' he said. 'You don't have to do anything but sit there with a book.'

'I didn't bring any books with me.'

'Then just enjoy the scenery. We're going to the next island west of here—Ikaria. Its name comes from Icarus.'

'The boy whose father made them wings to escape from prison, but he flew too high and the sun melted the wax on his wings and he drowned?'

'That's the one. Apparently he flew too high because he was so thrilled by the view—the mountains to the south, and fabulous beaches to the north.'

'How come you know about boats and the natural history around here?'

'I do occasionally take holidays.'

'And you've sailed before.'

'I learned in the same place as Admiral Nelson—the Norfolk Broads. If it was good enough for him...'

She smiled. 'That sounds like patter.'

'It is. But it's also true.' He smiled. 'Anyway, I knew you'd like this as you like things in shipshape order.'

She groaned. 'Your jokes are terrible.'

'I know.' He didn't look the slightest bit repentant. He carried their cases onto the yacht, then helped her on board. 'I just need to change, and then we'll go sailing and find a nice place to moor tonight. We can eat at a little taverna somewhere.'

She guessed he'd already researched the island and discovered the best places to eat.

'Just sit there and look at the boats for a minute. Oh, and change your shoes.' At her raised eyebrow, he spread his hands. 'Health and safety regulations.'

Now she knew why he'd told her to wear flat shoes. Not because they'd be walking, but because they'd be on a boat—and flat shoes with a decent grip were safer. 'My shoes are in my case,' she reminded him.

'Take those ones off—gorgeous though they are, I don't want you falling off the deck.' He blew her a kiss. 'I'll bring your sensible shoes up with me.'

When he reappeared, he was wearing a white shirt with the sleeves rolled halfway up his forearms, black chinos rolled up to his knees and deck shoes with no socks. He was also sporting dark glasses and a red bandana over his hair. 'Now, you have to imagine the earring, the parrot and the hook,' he said.

Her pirate fantasy. She loved the fact that he'd tried to indulge her; though she also knew he'd hate it if she went all gooey on him, so she resorted to sass. 'Captain Hook wore a pirate hat, not a bandana, and he had a red velvet coat,' she countered. 'Besides, pirate captains don't wear bandanas.'

'No?' He sat down beside her, placed her flat shoes on the deck and leaned over to kiss her thoroughly.

'You lied to me,' she said when she could catch her breath.

'How?'

'You told me we were going to Norfolk.'

'No. You assumed it. I just didn't correct you.'

'You lied about the reason why I needed a passport.'

'True, but it was a teensy fib to put you off the scent, purely because I wanted to surprise you. I'd never lie about anything important.'

She believed him. Luke was an honourable man. 'You'd never make a real pirate,' she said softly, stroking his face.

'Probably not. But, hey, I'm not the one with the Captain Hook fantasy.' He grinned. 'Oh, and for your information, pirate captains might wear bandanas if they're travelling incognito to do a bit of QC work in their fleet.'

She groaned. 'Please tell me this isn't work. You're not planning to buy a yacht? Or a spa hotel in Greece?'

'It's a thought…' Then he laughed. 'No, we're playing hooky for the weekend. Though there are various hot springs on the island. We can try them out, if you like. Or just moor at one of the harbours and paddle in the sea. Which reminds me.' He'd brought a bottle of sun cream up with the shoes. 'On a yacht, the sun's rays are reflected from the sea so they'll burn you more quickly. You need high protection factor.'

'Going to rub it on for me?' she teased.

'Now there's an offer. Be careful what you say to a pirate captain on a very secluded island,' he teased back. But he rubbed the cream into her skin, making sure it was thoroughly covered, before removing his bandana. 'I should've told you to bring a hat—I'll get you one when we moor, but in the meantime use this.'

'What about you?'

'Pirates don't need hats,' he said.

Sara felt slightly guilty, sitting there watching him do all the hard work of sailing the yacht, but as she knew practically nothing about boats she knew she'd just be in the way. Though she did enjoy the view: the blueness of the sea was stunning. And her view of the ship's pirate captain was even better.

He took her to Nas. 'Apparently, these are some of the best

ruins in Greece,' he informed her. 'There aren't that many of them—just the pier of the ancient port and the floor of the sanctuary dedicated to Artemis survive—but you get to see them in peace and quiet because they're off the beaten track. The villagers reused most of the stone in the church tower and in a stepping-stone bridge.'

'Have you been here before?' she asked, curious.

'No, I just read up about it. It's what made me decide to bring you here. I thought this would be the kind of place you'd like.'

She loved everything about Nas, from the beautiful cove with its soft, pale sand and clear blue water lapping at the shore, to the huge gorge with a river cutting through it, to the ruins themselves. And, when they followed the stream, they found a deep lake with a waterfall.

'This is too good to miss,' Luke said. He removed her shoes, kicked off his own, picked her up and walked straight into the lake.

'Luke!' she protested.

'We don't have any swimming things, and we'll be arrested if we skinny-dip. And I really, *really* want to kiss you under a waterfall,' he said. 'So this is the best option.'

'You're…you're…' she floundered.

'What?'

Gorgeous. Kind. Thoughtful. The man she'd lost her heart to. Not that she'd panic him by telling him so. 'Lovely,' she said.

'So are you.' He drew her over to the waterfall. 'Now kiss me.'

She did, and what started out as a warm, sweet kiss, silently telling him that she loved him, soon turned hot. To the point where they ended up running back to the yacht, and Luke made love to her thoroughly, jamming his mouth over hers to silence her cries of pleasure.

Afterwards, they found a sleepy taverna for a lunch of excellent grilled fish with herbs and salad, and tiny pastries dripping with honey.

Luke refused wine. 'Apart from the fact I'm crewing the boat so I need a clear head, I'm not a fan of retsina. But feel free to have what you like.'

She bit her lip. 'Luke, I feel bad about this. I don't have any local currency on me, and I want to pay for something.'

'Hey, I'm the one who stole your holiday in the first place. This is my way of making it up to you a little bit. Humour me.' He smiled at her. 'And to see you enjoying this is payment enough for me. Money isn't important.'

She coughed. 'Of course you can say that. It isn't an issue for you.'

'I came from nothing,' he said. 'And on the way I learned that money really *isn't* important. It's who you are inside that counts most.'

And Luke Holloway was a good man—one with a huge heart that he kept barricaded away. Though Sara was beginning to hope that he was slowly learning to trust her and would start dismantling the fences.

The weekend was magical, spent sailing round the island. They visited ruined castles and monasteries with beautiful frescoes and stunning views, bathed in the hot springs at Thermae, and late on Saturday they were awed to see a school of dolphins frolicking in the sea.

'That's just…' Words failed Sara and she simply slid her arm round Luke's waist, cuddling into him. He rested his arm on her shoulders and kissed the top of her head.

She had no idea how long they stayed there, just watching the dolphins arcing out of the water, but she was so glad she'd shared it with Luke. They moored overnight at another village, eating a simple yet beautifully cooked meal, and watched the sun set from the deck of the boat. The stars in Greece seemed bright and clear, like they never were in London, and, best of all, she fell asleep in Luke's arms that night.

Late on the Sunday afternoon, they flew back to London.

'It's late. Why don't you stay here tonight?' Luke suggested when they were back at his flat.

He'd never asked her to stay with him in London. Another barrier down? she wondered hopefully. 'I'll need to call Justin,' she said, 'just so he doesn't worry about whether we've had an accident on the way back.'

'Sure. I'll order us a takeaway.'

It felt oddly domesticated, eating pizza with Luke in his kitchen. Even more so, putting both their clothes in his washing machine. Though she knew better than to hope for too much, too soon. Right now, it was enough to lie in his arms in his enormous bed, watching the rain fall onto the windows and drifting off to sleep with her cheek pillowed against his heart.

CHAPTER THIRTEEN

ON THE Monday lunchtime, Sara headed over to Greenwich to buy Luke a gift to say thank you for the weekend. Knowing how much he hated clutter, she wanted to get him something useful, which meant something for his desk, but she also wanted it to be something that would remind him of a time when he'd actually relaxed.

In the third shop she tried, she found the perfect thing. And when Luke came back from a meeting, there was a box on his desk tied with blue ribbon.

'What's this?' he asked.

'For you,' she said, leaning back in her chair. 'Just to say thanks for the weekend.'

'You didn't have to buy me anything.'

'I wanted to.'

He untied the ribbon and removed the protective crumpled tissue paper, and simply stared.

'It's Swedish art glass,' she told him. 'A paperweight.' Two dolphins, sculpted from glass, encased in a wave of lead crystal.

'It's beautiful. You really didn't have to, but I appreciate it.'

He walked over to her desk, leaned over and kissed her. His kiss was warm and sweet; this was definitely more than just sexual attraction, Sara thought. And, although she didn't say it out loud, it felt a lot like love.

'I thought the dolphins might remind you of Ikaria. Though the island isn't just linked to Icarus, you know,' she said.

'Sounds as if someone's been doing some research,' he teased.

'I did. It's supposed to be the birthplace of Dionysus—and that's why it's linked to dolphins. When Dionysus was young, some pirates kidnapped him on his way to Naxos, so he stopped the ship and made vines grow over the sails. Then some beasts appeared as if by magic on the deck; the pirates jumped overboard in terror and they were changed into dolphins.'

'I'll think of you and your pirate fantasy whenever I look at it,' he said.

Luke asked her to stay over for two more nights that week; it convinced Sara that he was definitely letting down his barriers. So maybe, just maybe, if she asked him, he'd say yes…

'It's my niece's birthday on Sunday. I was wondering if you'd like to come with me?' she asked on the Friday morning. 'It's nothing elaborate because she's going to be two—just the usual family high tea and a birthday cake.'

'Family high tea.'

There was reservation in his tone, though when she looked at him his face was unreadable.

Clearly she'd pushed him too far, too fast. And hadn't he told her straight that he didn't like children? 'Look, you don't have to. It was just a thought. If you're not doing anything already.'

'It's nice of you to ask.'

She could hear the *but*. And she knew exactly what he was going to say because he always took refuge in work. Which meant she'd gone ten steps back instead of what she'd thought of as one tiny step forward.

'I…' He blew out a breath. 'OK. Sunday's fine.'

It was the last thing she'd expected him to say. So she just stared at him, stunned.

'But I don't exactly come across a lot of children in my line of work,' he added. 'You'll have to help me choose a present for her.'

'Present?'

'Even I know that you don't go to a party without a present for the birthday girl.' His tone was light, but his expression was till unreadable. She didn't have a clue what he was thinking, and it unsettled her.

He logged on to the Internet and typed in the name of the biggest toy shop in London—a name that was familiar even to people who didn't have children. 'What kind of things does she like?'

Then she realised. He was treating this as business; she knew this was his way of coping with things. She almost—*almost*—wrapped her arms round him and told him that everything was going to be fine, that all he had to do was tell her why families made him nervous, and she'd help him...but she didn't want to push him even further away. Look, I was going to hit the toy shop this evening. Why don't you come with me?'

'To the toy shop.' It was a statement rather than a question.

'Look, I know you've got something in your diary for late afternoon. Why don't I lock up here and we can meet at the corner of Regent Street and Oxford Circus at...say...six?'

He nodded and turned back to his desk. 'I'll call you if I'm running late.'

She couldn't leave it like this. 'Luke.'

'Mmm?' He looked up from the computer screen.

She laid her hand against his cheek. 'Thank you. I know this isn't really your kind of thing. I appreciate it.'

'No worries.' He made light of it, but his colour deepened. And her heart ached for him. What would it take to show him that he could trust her with himself? With his heart?

At precisely six o'clock, Luke met Sara in Regent Street and walked with her to the toy shop. It was full of families, parents choosing gifts for their children with love. How long had it been since he'd last set foot in a shop like this?

He pushed the thought away. Treat it like business, he told himself. Your goal is to choose a birthday gift for a small child. It's not difficult.

Though it *felt* difficult.

'Look at this.' Sara stood beside a carved wooden rocking horse with a mane and tail made of real hair. 'I always wanted something like this when I was little.'

Of course Sara would know exactly what a little girl would like. She'd been one herself. But he checked anyway. 'Do you think Maisie would like it?'

Her eyes widened. 'Luke, this costs a small fortune!'

He shrugged. 'It's only money.'

She looked away. 'It's nice of you, but…'

He read the answer in her face. 'Not appropriate for a two year-old? OK. I'm in your hands. You know what kind of things she'd like.' He just hoped that Sara wouldn't drag it out too long. This wasn't his idea of fun.

Eventually, they chose a bright pink easel, several non-spill pots of paint, chunky brushes that would be easy for small hands to hold and lots of paper.

'We're not taking this on the Tube,' he said as they left the shop. 'It's too bulky.' He hailed a taxi and gave the cab driver Justin's address.

'You're coming with me?' she asked, looking surprised when he slid into the back beside her.

'I'm hardly going to make you carry that lot up the stairs on your own,' he said mildly. 'Give me some credit.'

'I didn't mean that.' She bit her lip and took his hand. 'Just that I've already taken up a chunk of your evening.'

And she felt guilty about it? Ah, hell. Time to make a concession. 'I wasn't doing anything special. And if Justin's home maybe we can get a takeaway.'

Her smile was reward enough in itself. And sharing a curry and a beer with Sara, Justin and his new girlfriend, Zoe—a simple evening of good food, good music and a lot of affectionate teasing and laughter—Luke was shocked to find that he actually enjoyed it. Much, much more than he'd enjoyed the celebrity parties he used to attend.

Though his gut tightened on Sunday morning as they drew nearer to her family home. Nearer to being involved with a family again. Even though he was pretty sure that Sara's family was nothing like his own—he'd already met and liked Justin, and the rest of the Fleets were likely to be the same—the whole thing made him uneasy. It brought back memories he'd rather keep buried.

The driveway to the house was long and lined with trees. And the house at the end of it was stunning, a mix of honey- and rose-coloured bricks with well-proportioned sash windows. Two dormer windows nestled in the steeply pitched roof and there was a huge chimney at either end with a bowl-shaped top. No wonder Sara loved it here.

'How old is the house?' he asked.

'It's Queen Anne—so about three hundred years,' Sara said.

She directed him round the side of the house; there was a large gravelled area with several cars parked there, plus what looked like a stable block, an oast house and a huge barn. And, although the house hadn't looked that big from the front— three windows on the first floor and one either side of the front door—it went back a long way.

'Nobody ever uses the front door,' Sara said. 'Everyone always goes straight into the kitchen—it's the heart of the house.'

Remembering how much she enjoyed pottering around in his kitchen, he could well believe it. But, all the same, he was glad he was carrying the bulky presents for Maisie—presents that Sara had wrapped in sparkly paper and dressed up with a huge pink bow. Right at that moment, he felt that he could do with a little armour-plating.

Sara opened the door and four dogs—the ones in the pho- tographs in her flat—erupted. Two black Labradors, a Springer spaniel carrying a shoe and a Westie. Sara crouched down and they were all bouncing round her and licking her; she was laughing and not trying in the slightest to calm them down.

Then the spaniel spotted him and barked.

'Hey, it's OK. Luke's a friend,' she soothed.

Luke propped the presents against the wall, crouched down and put his hand out. The dog sniffed him and then licked his hand, before hunting round for the shoe he'd dropped earlier and dumping it at Luke's feet.

'Imelda, I presume?' he asked, laughing and retrieving the shoe before handing it to Sara.

'Yes. The Labradors are Russet and Pippin, and the Westie's Lamborne—Imelda was originally Bramley, until we discovered his shoe habit.'

'They're all named after varieties of apple?'

'What else would you expect, round here?' she teased back.

As she straightened up, an older woman joined them. Her resemblance to Sara was marked; seeing her was like seeing what Sara would be like in thirty years' time, Luke thought. Sara gave her mother a huge hug, then stepped back, grabbed Luke's hand and tugged him towards them. 'Luke, this is my mother, Nina Fleet—Mum, this is Luke Holloway.'

'Pleased to meet you, Luke,' Nina said politely.

'And you,' Luke said, holding out his hand.

To his shock, she didn't shake his hand; instead, she tutted, said, 'Oh, come here' and gave him a hug, too.

How many years had it been since he'd had a motherly hug?

Something inside him felt as if it had just cracked.

Part of him wanted to run. But the more sensible part of him knew that if he backed away it would hurt Sara. Nina Fleet was obviously the warm earth-mother type who greeted everyone with a hug. She was warm and plump and smelled of baking.

And, despite his reservations, Luke found himself returning her hug.

'Come in and have some coffee. Lamborne, get *down*. Pippin and Russet, stop pushing—there isn't room enough for both of you to get through the door at the same time as everyone else. And, Imelda, don't you even *think* about it,' Nina warned. 'Sara did tell you about not leaving your shoes anywhere, Luke?'

'Because Imelda will steal one and add it to his pile. Yes.'
He laughed, picked up the presents again and followed Nina
and Sara into the kitchen.

It was a proper farmhouse kitchen, with handmade cupboards painted cream, a scrubbed pine table and dresser, equally
scrubbed red tiles on the floor, two large wicker dog beds near
the Aga and a large butler's sink by the window with a view of
the orchard.

Luke fell in love with it instantly.

'There's a stack of presents in the living room—leave those
there, if you like, then come back and have a seat,' Nina said, ges-
turing to the table. 'I'm afraid it's a scratch lunch—jacket potatoes
and a casserole—because I've been baking all morning and there
just wasn't time to sort out a proper Sunday roast. But welcome,
anyway. Can I get you a mug of tea or would you prefer coffee?'

'Coffee would be lovely, thanks.'

Sara led him through to the living room—a large, airy room
with a huge open fireplace, comfortable sofas that were clearly
well used and just the right side of shabby and overfull book-
cases. There was a piano in the corner—the piano Sara had
learned to play as a child? he wondered—and there were
framed photographs everywhere. Weddings, babies, gradua-
tions, family get-togethers: they were all celebrated here.

A world away from what he was used to.

But at least Sara didn't push him to talk. She merely helped
him put the presents with the rest, then ushered him back to
the kitchen.

He noticed how Sara and her mother worked automatically
as a team; Sara fetched the cream-and-white-striped mugs and
matching sugar bowl while Nina shook grounds into a cafétière.
The next thing he knew, there was a steaming mug of coffee in
front of him, along with a plate containing a thick slice of warm
apple cake. 'Just to keep you going until lunch,' Nina added.

What a welcome. The Fleets were warm and trusting and
accepting, right from the start; from what he remembered of

his own childhood, everyone was suspect until proven and kept very firmly on the outside.

Probably one of the reasons why he was so suspicious of people in his personal life. It was inbred.

The dogs, who had been lying in their baskets, suddenly erupted again as a middle-aged man walked in, wearing faded jeans, muddy green wellington boots and a T-shirt with a faded slogan about apples.

This, Luke thought, must be Sara's father.

He removed the wellies and left them on the mat by the door. 'Imelda, leave,' he said firmly. The spaniel wagged his tail, as if to ask how anyone could possibly think he'd be naughty enough to run off with a single green wellie. Then the man enveloped his daughter in a huge hug, kissing her soundly. 'And how many pairs of shoes have you bought this week, darling?'

'None. I'm not *that* bad.'

'No?' he teased.

'No.' Sara laughed and hugged him back. 'Dad, this is Luke.'

He strode over to the table and held out his hand. 'Nice to meet you. I'm James.'

'Luke.'

The older man's handshake was firm and dry, and Luke's gut feeling told him that James Fleet was one of the good guys.

This was going to be all right.

The house filled up before lunch—which was a fabulous meal, and very far from being the 'scratch lunch' Nina had described it as—and then, just as Nina was shooing them from the kitchen, Louisa arrived with her husband, Bryan, and his parents.

'And here's the birthday girl,' Nina cooed.

The little girl toddled in and hugged everyone in turn; clearly she was as tactile as the rest of the Fleets, Luke thought.

But she stopped dead in front of Luke and looked up at him, eyes wide.

Of course. He was a stranger.

Dangerous.

Sara scooped the little girl up and lifted her so she was nearer Luke's height. 'Maisie, sweetheart, this is my friend Luke,' she said.

Friend, Luke thought. Well. *Lover* wasn't an appropriate word to use to a child. But *friend*… The idea warmed him and scared him in equal measure.

'Lulu,' Maisie pronounced, testing the word. Then she beamed, and a pair of chubby hands seized Luke's arm. 'Lulu.'

Help. He had no idea what to say. And he was well aware that everyone was watching him. Well, he'd pretend this was business. Be nice. Be charming. 'Hello, Maisie. Happy birthday.'

The little girl beamed again. ''Lo, Lulu.'

Sara chuckled. 'You're going to have a hard time living that name down. And what's it worth not to mention it to any of your business associates back in London?'

'How about not smuggling Imelda back to London in the back of my car, and letting him loose among your shoes?' Luke retorted.

Everyone laughed, and it felt as if he'd passed some kind of test. Yet he still found himself on edge. The bond between Sara and her family was close and deep—a world in which he didn't really belong. So much for thinking he could handle this. Even treating it like a business deal didn't make it feel any better.

Luke did his best to smile and be charming, joining in with the birthday tea and singing *Happy birthday to you* along with everyone else when Rupert sat down at the piano and Sara and Justin stood either side of him, adding in extra harmonies. But he was relieved when the presents were unwrapped and the birthday cake candles were blown out and Louisa and Bryan took their sleepy daughter home for bath and bedtime—especially when Sara suggested they needed to start heading back to London.

She'd clearly noticed that he'd gone quiet because, on the way back, she said, 'Luke? I didn't mean to offend you, you know. When Maisie called you Lulu—you know what kids are like.'

Actually, he didn't.

'Maisie has a brilliant vocabulary for her age, but your name was a new word to her. If it makes you feel any better, she calls Justin "Jussie".'

'It's fine,' Luke said.

'Then what's wrong?'

'Nothing,' he lied, not wanting to hurt her. He had to find the right words to tell her—if he really got involved with her, he'd have to open his life up to a family, do what he'd spent all his life avoiding. And he wasn't sure he could do it. 'I'm just a bit tired, that's all.'

Sara wasn't convinced. Clearly there was something in Luke's past that he wasn't telling her. He'd closed up again, and the only thing she could think of that had changed since the previous day was that he'd met her family.

So didn't he like them?

She couldn't imagine why anyone wouldn't like the Fleets. Even Hugh had liked them—before he'd betrayed them.

But why else would Luke be so quiet?

She hoped he wouldn't expect her to choose between them. It would be like being ripped apart; she phoned her mother and Louisa a couple of times a week, emailed Rupert, texted her Dad, had breakfast with Justin…not a day went past when she wasn't in contact with at least two members of her family. No way would she give them up.

On the other hand…she didn't want to give Luke up, either.

She just wanted him to love her family, the way she did. The way they'd love him, if he let them.

Finally, Luke pulled up outside the flat.

'Do you want to come in for a coffee?' she asked.

'Thanks, but I'll take a rain check. I'm a bit tired, and there are a couple of things I need to sort out before the morning.'

'OK. See you tomorrow.'

She kissed him on the cheek, and noted miserably that he didn't kiss her back.

Maybe he'd talk to her tomorrow. Maybe.

But she slept badly that night. And, when she walked into the office, Luke was talking on the phone, only having time to wave an acknowledgement to her. Fair enough—he was running a business—but when he replaced the receiver she noticed that he didn't kiss her hello.

He didn't kiss her goodbye when he left for a meeting, either. So what did this mean? They were back to being just business associates?

It looked as if she was going to have to play this by ear. Take it step by step. And hope that he'd let her get close enough to tell her what was going on in his head.

'Are you all right?' Luke asked when he came back into the office.

'Sure. Why?'

'You're a bit quiet.'

Sara shrugged. 'You haven't been here most of the day.'

'Because there's been a problem at one of the gyms. Suspected subsidence. I needed to talk to a surveyor, and discuss with the manager how we can minimise disruption to the clients.' He shrugged. 'Things happen.'

'Mmm.'

He felt his eyes narrow. 'Sara? I'm not a mind-reader. Spit it out.'

'What's wrong with my family?' she asked.

He blinked. Talk about out of left field. 'Nothing.'

'But you didn't like them, did you?'

'Of course I did. I get on all right with Justin, don't I?'

She folded her arms. 'So why did you go all distant on me yesterday?'

How on earth could he explain that? Not without dragging up a lot of stuff from his past that was best left where it belonged. In the past. 'You're overreacting, Sara.'

'Am I?'

He sighed. 'Look. I admit, I find families difficult.'

'If mine were all selfish monsters, like some of my friends' families are, I could understand it. Of course you'd want to avoid them. But my family are *nice*, Luke. They're decent, kind people who put themselves in other people's shoes.'

Decent and kind. 'Not everyone has a family like that.' His certainly wasn't.

She picked up on it immediately. 'So yours are monsters? That's rough, and you have my sympathy—and I do mean sympathy, Luke, not pity. But it still doesn't mean you have to cut yourself off from everyone else.'

'You're making me sound unreasonable.'

'Because you *are* being unreasonable, Luke.'

'I'm a bit wary, that's all.'

She scoffed. 'That's the understatement of the century.'

'I'm sorry. I'll try, OK? But…look, it's not easy for me. Don't expect too much.' He glanced at his watch. 'I have to be elsewhere, and I probably won't be back before you leave tonight. But we'll talk later, yes?'

'Yes.'

Except he didn't finish until it was way too late to call her. He sent her an apologetic text as a stopgap, and in the morning he called in to a florist's he knew opened early. She'd liked the last flowers he'd bought her, and in his experience this was the best way to defuse a fight.

And, although he was sitting at his desk when Sara walked in, pretending to be absorbed in a spreadsheet, inside he was as jumpy as hell.

She took one look at the hand-tied arrangement of pale pink roses, lilac alstroemeria and silvery-green eucalyptus foliage sitting on her desk and her eyes narrowed. 'What are these for?'

'To say sorry.'

Her mouth thinned. 'I don't need gestures, Luke. I just wanted you to talk to me, so I could understand what's going on in your head.'

'I told you, I have issues.'

She came to sit on the edge of his desk. 'Then tell me. Why do you have such a problem with families?'

'I don't want to talk about it.'

She folded her arms. 'So we're back to square one.'

She really wasn't going to let him off the hook, was she? 'Not everyone gets on with their family,' he said carefully.

'Agreed.'

'I haven't seen mine for a lot of years. We don't have anything in common.'

'No. I guess we're not all millionaires,' she said dryly.

That stung. He lifted his chin. 'It's got nothing to do with money. I didn't have a lot when I left. Just a suitcase of clothes and my share in the market stall.' He stared at her. 'I thought you knew me better than that. I don't judge people on how much they earn or how much they have in the bank.'

'So what do you judge them on?'

'I told you before. Who they are. How they treat other people. And my family…' He sucked in a breath. 'I really don't want to talk about this. Let's just leave it that they don't see things the way I do.'

She looked thoughtful. 'That happens in a lot of families, and it's sad, but sometimes it's the best thing for everyone concerned.'

Relief flooded through him. Thank God. She understood.

And then she looked straight at him. 'But you're using it as an excuse to cut yourself off from the human race, Luke, and that's not good at all.'

'I'm not cutting myself off from the human race.'

'But you don't get involved.'

'Correct.'

'Well, at least I know where I stand.' She slid off his desk and went back over to hers. And although she placed the flowers very carefully on top of the filing cabinets, where they couldn't accidentally be knocked over, he knew that he'd done the wrong thing. Instead of fixing it, he'd made things worse because he'd tried to fob her off with a gesture. One that would've worked on any of his previous girlfriends—but Sara wasn't like them. Money and possessions—except, possibly, shoes—weren't important to her.

She was quiet for the rest of the day, and Luke felt more and more of a heel—and more and more at a loss how to fix this.

At precisely five o'clock she switched off her computer.

'Sara. Have dinner with me tonight?'

'Thanks for the offer, but I'm a bit tired.'

'Look, I can skip my squash. We could eat earlier. Whatever time you like.' He was offering her time, for pity's sake. Wasn't that what she wanted from him?

'Thanks, but I really need an early night.'

In other words, she was still angry with him and wanted some space.

On Tuesday, Luke was out of the office for most of the day and Sara had left before he returned. There was a note on his desk saying that she'd worked through lunch and left three-quarters of an hour early and she hoped he didn't mind.

He did mind.

A lot.

They couldn't carry on like this. Apart from anything else, he missed her.

She was probably on the Tube now, he thought, so there was no point in calling. He left enough time to allow her to get to Camden tube station, then called her mobile.

For a nasty moment, he thought she was going to let it go through to voice mail. Then she answered. 'Hello?'

'Hi. It's Luke.' Stupid—she would already know that from the caller display. 'Um…are you busy this evening?' And then he remembered. Of course she was. Tuesday night was her regular night out with the girls.

Her next words confirmed it. 'I'm going to the cinema with Liz and Sophie. And then we're going to an ice cream parlour.'

'Uh-huh.' He chose his words carefully. 'Maybe afterwards you could come here. I could make you a hot chocolate or something.'

'A hot chocolate.'

'The offer's there. I'll leave it up to you. Enjoy your film.'

'Thanks.'

She didn't make any promises to call in later, and Luke couldn't settle to anything for the rest of the evening. Just when he thought that she'd decided to go back to her own flat, his entryphone buzzed.

'This hot chocolate had better be good,' a voice informed him.

'It will be.' He buzzed her in.

She looked slightly wary when she walked in the door. He said nothing, just walked over to meet her, wrapped his arms round her and buried his face in her shoulder.

Just breathing in her scent calmed him; finally, he lifted his head. 'I'm sorry. I'll try harder. I did like your family.'

'You just have...issues.'

'Yeah. Like you said, there are people, and there are not-so-nice people. People I don't want to be part of. It's in the past now. And that's where I want it to stay—where I need it to stay.'

In answer, she stroked his face. Brushed her mouth against his. 'Just don't shut me out again, Luke.'

'I'll try. Believe me, I'll try,' he promised. And he meant it.

CHAPTER FOURTEEN

FOR the next couple of weeks, all was fine in Sara's world. More nights than not, she stayed overnight at Luke's flat, and he didn't seem to mind when she filled his fridge and pottered around in his kitchen. He even made the effort to go with her to see her family again.

Although neither of them said anything, she knew how she felt about him.

And she thought she knew how he felt about her.

It was more than just sex. Much more.

But then she had a phone call that worried her sick. To the point where she was so quiet at work that at half past nine on the Friday morning Luke turned off her computer screen and sat on the edge of her desk.

'Hey! I was in the middle of a report,' she protested.

'I don't care. Talk to me,' he said.

'What about?'

'Whatever's bothering you. And don't say it's nothing. You haven't been yourself all week.'

She shook her head. 'It's family stuff.'

'You've fallen out with them?'

'No, of course not.'

'Then what?' He reached over to take her hand and squeezed it briefly. 'Sara, things can't be that bad.'

'They are.' She sighed. 'When things go wrong with old houses it takes loads of time and tons of cash.'

'And there's something wrong with your parents' house?' he guessed.

'The roof. That summer storm the other week blew a few tiles off.' She bit her lip. 'Dad thought it was fixable, but when the builder came round to look at it, he found they've got dry rot in the timbers. It's not covered by the insurance and it's going to cost a fortune to fix.'

'Ah.'

'The problem is, all Mum and Dad's money is tied up in the business and, with the cost of everything going up, there just isn't the cashflow to deal with it. Not with something this big.' She bit her lip. 'I've got some savings, but Rupert's halfway through buying a house himself and Lou's expecting again so she and Bryan are too stretched to help. Justin tried to remortgage his flat to release some equity, but all the lenders wanted to know why he wants the extra money. And when they found out, all of them said no.' She dragged in a breath. 'Which means Mum and Dad will have to sell the business—because no way is anyone going to give them a decent price for a house with dry rot. And the orchard's been in our family for years and years. Since my great-great-grandfather's day. It'll kill Dad to lose it. Especially after—' She stopped abruptly. Luke didn't need to know about the business with Hugh.

'After what?'

'Doesn't matter.'

'Hey. You told me not to shut you out. It goes both ways.'

She was silent for a long, long time. Luke sighed, scooped her out of her chair, sat down in her place and settled her on his lap. 'Right. Talk.'

'Hugh,' she said finally.

'The workaholic?'

She nodded. 'I thought he loved me. Thought he liked my

family. And Mum and Dad were going to expand, float th
business on the stock market.'

He stroked her hair. 'What happened?'

'It turned out that Hugh had been advising a consortium—
people who cared about profit, not about what my parents wer
trying to do. They made a hostile takeover bid. Dad just abou
managed to stave it off, but he and Mum lost a lot of mone
through it. So it's my fault they don't have the funds to cove
the roof repairs.'

'No, it's not.'

'If it wasn't for me introducing him to them, Hugh wouldn'
have known.'

'Actually, if he was in the speculative money markets, i
would've been his job to know who was floating. The fact h
knew you is completely irrelevant. So it *wasn't* your fault.' H
gritted his teeth. 'Only a first-class bastard would use you lik
that—and then make you take the blame.' Luke's fists tight
ened; he had to make a real effort to relax them. 'Violenc
doesn't solve anything, but right now I'd like to wipe th
floor with him.'

'He isn't worth it.'

'No, but you are.' He leaned forward to brush his mout
against hers. 'Right. There's no point sitting here worrying.
need the facts.'

'What do you mean?'

'It's what I do. Turn businesses round. If your parents wi
trust me to look at their books and talk me through what the
do and how, I might be able to come up with a solution.'

'You'd help them? For me?'

'It's business. What I do,' he said coolly.

She damped down the flare of hurt.

'And I'm not Hugh, if that's what you're worrying about.'

'I know you're not.'

'Good. So I suggest you ring your parents and see if we ca
go down now.'

'Now?' She stared at him in surprise. 'But you've got meetings.'

'Nothing in my diary is set in stone. You can rearrange my schedules while I'm driving. Say something important's cropped up.'

'You'd really do that?' For her? And he'd been the one to make the suggestion, not her. A warm glow of hope filled her.

'I owe you,' he said. 'You've made me reassess my priorities and learn to fill the well.'

She frowned. 'You don't owe me anything.' Relationships didn't work that way.

'OK. You've also helped me out of a hole and you've let me dragoon you into staying on as my PA.'

'Until you find a temp. And the fact you haven't done so yet, I might add, means you're either too fussy or you're slacking.'

He smiled. 'When you're sassy with me, I know all's right with the world. Ring your parents.'

So now he knew exactly what had happened to make Sara wary of relationships, Luke thought grimly as he drove down the motorway. Someone who'd taken advantage of her good nature, through her most vulnerable spot: her family.

Though wasn't he just as bad as Hugh, in his own way? He was taking advantage of her, too. True, he was planning to help her family out of a hole rather than put them in one—it was the best way he knew to pay Sara back for what she'd given him. But he also knew what she wanted in life. Someone who'd love her. Who'd love her family. Without reserve.

Could he do that?

He wasn't sure.

So it was unfair to keep her hanging on. He really ought to do the right thing: say goodbye, give her the chance of finding someone who deserved her. Someone who'd be able to give her what she needed. Someone…who wasn't him.

And that was the problem.

He didn't want it to be someone else.

But, at the same time, he couldn't get past his wariness o
family. Sara wanted children—she'd told him that. The idea o
being a father scared the hell out of him. She'd grown up in suc
different circumstances from his. How would he ever be abl
to give her the things she needed, the things she was used to
Things that couldn't be fixed by a business deal?

'So how much has Sara filled you in on the situation?' Jame
asked when Luke was sitting at the kitchen table, nursing a mu
of Nina's excellent coffee and with Imelda lying on his feet.

'Expensive roof repairs plus the credit crunch,' Luke said
'and you don't want to sell the business to people who don'
have the same ethics that you do and are in it because they'r
jumping on a bandwagon, not because they care.'

'Got it in one.' James looked grim. 'My family's had thi
orchard for four generations—five, if you count Ruper
coming in on sales and Lou doing the office. And I don't wan
to lose it.'

And it wasn't just financial, Luke knew. The business wa
something he cared about. Was part of the family history. Hel
their roots.

He'd walked away from his family's business. He wasn'
going to walk away from Sara's. 'Take me through the busines
and show me what you do, then we'll look at figures.'

James nodded. 'Look, it's not especially boggy in th
orchard, but the grass is long enough and wet enough to mes
up your shoes. I don't suppose you brought wellies with you?

'I didn't even think about it,' Luke admitted.

'Not a problem. We have spares for visitors to use. Com
with me and we'll sort you out. Do you mind some of the dog
coming with us?'

'No, it's fine.' Luke couldn't ever remember having a pe
not even a goldfish. And noisy, muddy dogs who insisted o
sitting as close to you as they could, or trotting along besid

you and nudging your knees every so often, were way out of his ken. But, to his surprise, he rather liked it.

James pulled on his boots again. 'Then let's be going. See you lot later.' He kissed his wife and ruffled both daughters' hair. When they'd left the kitchen, he said softly to Luke, 'I hope you can do something because it'll break Nina's heart if we have to give this up. I would consider selling the house, but in this economic climate it'd be hard to get a buyer, and selling wouldn't change the fact that the roof has dry rot and it's going to cost a small fortune to sort it.'

'I've worked with businesses on the edge of bankruptcy,' Luke said, 'and we've managed to turn it around.'

'By getting rid of half the staff and making the others take up the slack?'

'No. I admit I've had to trim hours back in some places, but if your team's all on the same side and they know you're going to be honest with them, people will be flexible. And once you're out of the rough patch, you make sure everyone shares in the smooth again.'

James gave him a considering look. 'So you're suggesting maybe employee shares?'

'I'll need to look at figures before I say anything. But talk me through the orchard and the factory, and we'll take it from here,' Luke said.

Apart from a brief lunch of home-made soup, home-made bread rolls, tangy Cheddar and apple chutney, eaten round the table with Sara, Louisa and Nina, Luke spent most of the day with James, looking at figures. And, at the end of the day, Nina insisted that they stay for dinner.

'If I'd known we were staying, I would've brought some wine and chocolates as my contribution,' Luke said.

'Don't be silly.' Nina shook her head. 'You've already done enough—you've given up today to work with us. Now, go and sit in the dining room, you lot.'

The house had filled up since lunchtime, Luke thought.

Rupert, the baby of the family, was there with his fiancée, Emmy. Louisa's husband, Bryan, had joined them, along with little Maisie, who insisted on sitting on his lap and kept patting his arm and saying, 'Lulu.'

A big, noisy family who talked a lot and laughed even more. A family who did things *together*. A family who listened to what he had to say about the business and then leapt straight into a full-blown discussion, with ideas bounced off each other and suggestions and offers of help.

The one thing that came out loud and clear was how much they loved each other. Sara offered to take a sabbatical from her business to help her family set up an online shop and to put her savings into converting some of the disued barns into holiday cottages, Rupert offered to put his house-buying on hold and put his deposit into kitting out the holiday cottages, and Louisa knew several other local businesses that would give them reciprocal links to an online shop, through her contacts at Maisie's nursery. Justin intended to call in favours to get all the legal work done for nothing.

And that was when it really hit Luke.

This was a family who really supported each other. And he was absolutely certain that Sara's parents had shown that same support to their children when it had been needed; neither Sara nor Justin worked in the family business, but he'd guess they'd never been pressured to change their career choices to fit in.

This was something, he was beginning to realise, that was worth more than any of the huge business deals he'd done in the past. A family that cared.

He was very quiet for the rest of the evening, letting them do the talking.

'It's getting late,' Nina said. 'Stay the night. It won't take me a second to make up the guest room.'

'That's really kind of you, Nina, but I'm sorry, I can't. I have some early meetings tomorrow.'

'If you're sure? You're not putting us out.'

'I'm sure. But thank you. The offer's appreciated.'

Sara saw him outside.

'Are you staying?' he asked. 'Because if you want to stay that's fine.'

She looked torn. 'I want to be with you,' she said, 'but right now I think my family needs me most. We have a lot to discuss.'

'Sure, I understand.' And he wasn't going to make her choose between them. But the drive back to London that evening was lonely and the car felt empty, even though he filled it with loud music. When he walked into his flat, its clean uncluttered spaciousness somehow felt sterile.

And Luke dearly wished he'd accepted the invitation to stay and be part of them, even if it was only for a little while.

CHAPTER FIFTEEN

OVER the next three weeks, with Luke's full agreement, Sara cut down her hours working with him and spent half her time in Kent and half her time in London.

At the end of the first week, he gave her a key to his flat. 'This isn't a statement of intent,' he warned, 'and we're not living together exactly, but I was thinking… If you stay here while you're in London, then at least we'll get to see something of each other.'

Sara thought it was as near as a man like Luke was ever going to get to a declaration of intent, and she was happy with that. Even better, Luke unbent enough to spend Sundays with her family, and he really did muck in with everyone else, insisting on doing the washing up and carrying things through to the dining table. He always brought her mother flowers, spent time talking business with her father—and then walked hand in hand with her in the orchard after lunch, kissing her next to every tree.

'You really need to be here at apple blossom time,' Sara said. 'It's lovely; you lie looking up at the trees, and the blossom floats down like—' She stopped the word in time, but she knew he'd guessed what she'd almost said.

Confetti.

He let it pass, but she was aware he'd quietly put a barrier up. On the Wednesday night of the third week, she got up at

tupid o'clock, feeling queasy. It must, she thought, have been
omething she'd eaten. She sipped a glass of cold water, very
lowly, and told herself she'd be fine in the morning.

Except she wasn't. The queasiness didn't pass during the
lay. And, worse still, it suddenly hit her that her period was late.

It couldn't be.

She was always regular, always twenty-eight days on the dot.
A swift calculation told her she was three days late. And she
hadn't noticed because she'd been rushing around between
Kent and London.

She and Luke hadn't taken any risks—they'd always been
scrupulous about using condoms—so she was pretty sure it was
caused by stress, worrying about her parents and the orchard.
But all the same she decided to take a pregnancy test. It was
bound to be negative, but she knew that actually seeing a
negative result would help to settle her fears.

Luckily Luke was in a meeting so she had time to buy it
without him knowing. She didn't want to tell him because she
knew how he felt about having children; although he seemed
to have softened a bit since meeting her family, she knew that
most of his barriers were still there and she wasn't going to take
anything for granted.

She bought a digital test, read the instructions and headed
for the bathroom. Once she'd done the test, she sat watching
the window on the test stick. The window was flashing,
showing that the test was working. Any minute now, the con-
firmation would come up: *Not Pregnant*. Any minute now.

And then the screen changed.

It really couldn't be any clearer.

Pregnant.

Sara stared at it, horrified. Pregnant? How on earth was she
going to tell Luke? He had issues about families as it was; he
still hadn't told her the whole story, but she guessed his
problems lay with his experiences as a child.

And if she told him she was expecting their baby—that he

was going to be part of a family again, whether he liked it or not—how was he going to react? Would he be pleased? Would he be horrified? Would he retreat even further behind his barriers?

She had no idea.

She knew without having to ask that her family would be supportive. But the important one here was Luke. Would this be the one thing that pushed him away from her completely?

She couldn't think straight; her head felt fuzzy. And maybe it was the power of suggestion, but she was promptly sick.

'You look a bit pale,' Luke said when he returned to the office.

'I'm fine,' Sara said, giving him a smile that he thought was a little too bright.

He wasn't so sure. She'd been under a lot of strain lately, worrying about her parents and the orchard. 'Look, if you've got a headache, don't just sit there and struggle on. Take the afternoon off. Go upstairs and have a nap or something. There's some paracetamol in the medicine kit in the kitchen—it's the green box under the sink.'

'I'm fine. I don't need a nap.'

But, a few moments later, she bolted from the room, her hand over her mouth.

An autumn virus, maybe?

But Luke had a bad feeling about this. It was too reminiscent of the way Di had behaved in the early stages of her pregnancy, looking tired and pale, and then rushing from the room to be sick.

Could Sara be pregnant?

They'd always been careful. Always used a condom.

But supposing one had split and he hadn't noticed?

Then again, some couples spent months trying to make a baby. For Sara to be pregnant after just one accident, well, it was pretty unlikely.

Unlikely...but not impossible.

Was Sara expecting his baby?

His head spun. It was the worst possible thing that could happen.

He didn't want children. Never had, never would.

How could he possibly be a good father? His own had let him down. And, no matter how hard Luke tried to avoid it, he knew he'd end up following the pattern. It was inbuilt. He'd let his child down. Let Sara down.

And another deeper fear crept in. Would Sara let him down? If he took the risk and let her through his last barrier, let himself believe in families again…what if it went wrong?

He didn't think he could walk away intact this time.

Hell, hell, hell.

This was a nightmare.

But it was one he was going to have to face head-on.

Sara walked back into the office, and her face was even paler. He fetched her a glass of water.

'Thank you.' This time, her smile was slightly wobbly.

He stayed where he was, in front of her desk. 'I think we need to talk.' He folded his arms. 'Is there anything you want to tell me?'

'Such as?'

Might as well ask her straight. 'Were you throwing up just now?'

She closed her eyes. 'It's probably a virus.'

'Sara. Look at me.'

She did so, and sighed. 'All right. Yes. I'm pregnant. I don't know how pregnant—I only did the test today.'

The world spun and he felt sick. 'And you never even thought to tell me you suspected it?'

'I didn't. Not until today. When I started feeling sick and realised my period's a few days late. I thought it was stress, but I wanted to be sure.' She dragged in a breath. 'That test was meant to reassure me that I'm *not* pregnant.'

He knew he ought to be kind. That he ought to hold her and tell her he'd support her. But fear pushed him into snapping at her. 'How?'

'How do you think babies are made, Luke?' she sniped back.

'I know that. I meant how, when we were always careful to use a condom?'

'I don't know.' She looked wearily at him. 'I suppose I should be grateful that you're not questioning whether it's yours.' Her eyes narrowed. 'At least, I *hope* you're not.'

'Of course I'm not,' he snapped. It hadn't even occurred to him.

All he could focus on was the fact that he was going to be a father.

That he didn't know *how* to be a father.

That this was a monumental mess.

'I'll do the right thing by you,' he said, looking away.

'What?'

'Marry you.'

And then the phone rang. He stomped over to his desk, grateful for the diversion, and picked it up. 'Luke Holloway.'

Just what he needed. A problem with a contract that his solicitor needed to discuss with him. The timing couldn't have been better. 'OK. I'll be there. Twenty minutes.' He replaced the receiver. 'I have to go. Legal stuff. I'll be back later—we'll talk then. Leave a message on my mobile's voice mail if anything crops up.'

And then he walked out of the office. Into the fresh air. Where, just for a few seconds, he could breathe again.

Luke could see that Sara was spoiling for a fight the minute he walked back into the office. Her face was tight with tension, and she was slamming her fingers onto the keyboard instead of using her usual light touch.

'Hi,' he said.

She lifted her chin. 'Where the hell have you been?'

'Sorting out legal stuff. As you know.'

'And it didn't occur to you to call me or text me, let me know you were on your way back?'

It had. He'd decided against it; the kind of conversation he'd known he'd face was the sort that was much better conducted face to face. 'What's the problem?'

'What's the *problem*?' She shook her head in apparent disbelief. 'I tell you I'm pregnant, and you tell me you'll do the right thing by me.'

He spread his hands. 'What did you want me to do? Tell you that you were on your own?'

'It's the way you did it, Luke. You didn't even *look* at me when you talked about marriage. And you couldn't wait to get away. If I were the paranoid type, I'd say that you rigged that call from your solicitor. It couldn't have come at a more perfect time for you.'

'Apart from the fact I had no idea what you were going to tell me,' he reminded her, 'you're perfectly at liberty to call my solicitor and check where I've been. I don't have any reason to lie to you, Sara.' He tossed his mobile phone over to her. 'Here. Check the call list.'

'I don't need to check the call list!' She threw it back at him. Hard.

'Don't you think you're being a bit—' He stopped abruptly, seeing real anger in her face.

'Don't you *dare* accuse me of being hormonal, Luke Holloway. It's got nothing to do with that. It's the fact that you're so bloody compartmentalised. You're emotionally lacking.'

There wasn't anything he could say to that. Because he knew it was true.

'Luke, I'm pregnant. With our child. Doesn't that mean anything to you?'

'Of course it does. I told you I'd marry you. I'll put your name on the deeds of the flat along with mine. It's up to you whether you want to carry on working after the baby's born; if you don't want to, then that's fine—I'll add your name to my bank account and I'll make sure you're not short of money.' It was the perfect deal.

'It's got nothing to do with money! What about your time, Luke?'

'Time?'

'Time. Are you going to cut down your working hours to spend time with me and our baby?'

'I…' He faltered.

'I thought not. You can't run my life, or our child's, like the way you run a business. Life doesn't *work* like that. And if you can't see that…' She gave him a look of utter disgust, picked up her handbag and slammed the office door behind her. Hard.

Luke dropped into his chair. He'd give her a couple of days to calm down and see sense and then he'd go and fetch her. Talk it over rationally. Get her to see that he'd given her the perfect offer.

But in the meantime he needed a temp to keep things ticking over. Sighing, he picked up the phone and dialled the agency's number. Arranged for someone to come in, first thing in the morning.

Although he worked until his eyes ached, he couldn't settle that evening and he slept badly that night. It didn't feel right, not having Sara next to him. He missed the warmth of her body against his.

The kitchen didn't feel right, either.

Or the living room.

Everything felt very slightly out of shape. As if it didn't fit him any more.

Which was ridiculous.

He lasted three days before he called her again. Her mobile phone was switched off, the phone in Justin's flat seemed to be permanently on answering machine and she didn't return a single one of his texts. By the time Luke was meant to meet Karim on the Monday evening, he was in a seriously foul temper.

And then Karim said something that took the wind out of his sails completely.

'Guess what we did today?'

'Aired your flat after a month away in Harrat Salma?' Luke guessed.

'Nope.' Karim fished his wallet out of his pocket and drew something out of it. 'Look.'

It was a photograph. Most of it was black, but there was a triangular-shaped swathe showing the outline of a baby's head and curled-up body.

'It's the twenty-week scan of your honorary nephew-to-be,' Karim announced, beaming.

Luke couldn't help himself.

He flinched.

His best friend noticed immediately. 'Right. We're not playing squash. And I don't care if the court's booked or not. I think you need to talk.'

'I…' His protest died. 'Not here.' Not here, where they might be overheard.

Karim's eyes narrowed. 'When did you last eat?'

'Breakfast. I think.' Luke couldn't recall. And he didn't really care.

'Right.' Karim shepherded him out of the health club and into the small pizzeria round the corner. Being a Monday night, it was quiet and they managed to find a table right out of the way. Karim ordered for them both and kept the conversation light until they'd finished the pizza and were both drinking coffee. 'Now, talk,' he said.

'Can I ask you a weird question?'

Karim frowned but nodded. 'Sure.'

'When Lily told you she was pregnant…how did you feel?' Luke asked.

Karim's eyes widened. 'Are you saying…?'

'Don't answer a question with a question. I really need to know.' To know he wasn't the only one who felt that way, to know he wasn't going crazy. 'What was your first reaction—your very first reaction?'

'Shock, I suppose. Because we hadn't really been trying—and, to be honest, I'd wanted a bit more time with her just as a couple. But then it sank in.' Karim smiled. 'There's going to be someone else in this world like Lily—someone else I know I'm going to love from his very first second in this world.'

'So you were pleased?'

'And proud. And, I suppose, a bit scared. I haven't exactly spent a lot of time around babies. How will I know if I'm a good enough father?'

His best friend had the same doubts? But that was crazy. Karim would make a fabulous father. 'You'll be great. You've got the example of your own father,' Luke reminded him.

Karim looked thoughtful. 'So is Sara pregnant?'

Luke sighed heavily. 'Yes. And I reacted badly when she told me.'

'Ouch.'

Luke stared bleakly at his best friend. 'The way you said you felt—that's how I felt, too. Shocked. And scared.'

'And pleased?'

Luke shook his head. 'Right now, I still can't get past the fear.'

Karim paused. 'You've never told me the whole story, and I'm not going to pry. But the fact you were strong enough to walk away from your family…that tells me you're going to be strong enough to be a good father. That you'll be the father to your child that you never had yourself.'

'That very much depends,' Luke said dryly, 'on whether I get the chance to do that.'

'Sara's not speaking to you?'

'No. Her mobile's permanently switched off and she won't answer my calls. And, for the first time in my life, I honestly don't know how to fix this.'

Karim patted his shoulder. 'The only thing you can do is be yourself. Tell her how you really feel. Open up to her.'

Luke shook his head. 'I don't do open.'

'Neither did I—until Lily,' Karim replied. 'If Sara's the one, you'll know. Because it'll be much harder being without her than with her.'

'Without her, it feels as if the world's turned grey,' Luke admitted. 'Nothing fits any more.'

'Then she's the one,' Karim said. 'Talk to her. What's the worst that can happen?'

'She turns me down.' Luke gave a mirthless laugh. 'Well, she's already done that. I told her I'd do the right thing and marry her.'

'Because of the baby?'

'Yes.'

Karim sucked in a breath. 'Ouch. If I'd done that to Lily, she would've walked out on me. Sara needs to know that you want her—'

'—for herself,' Luke finished. 'Yeah. I just worked that out. I have a lot of humble pie to eat.' He drained his coffee. 'Thanks for the advice.'

'Let me know how it goes.'

'Yeah.' Luke wasn't even sure that Sara was going to talk to him. But he was prepared to do whatever it took to turn things around and make a real future with Sara and their baby.

But first he had to talk to her.

And he had to convince her that he was telling the truth.

Luke knew that if he turned up with a ring or a huge bouquet, Sara would reject them—and him. He needed to make her see that he meant it, that he really did want to be a family with her. Which meant giving her something that money couldn't buy.

On his way back to his flat, he walked past a mother-and-baby shop. In the middle of the window display was a baby book, its pages open; he glanced at it and realised it was meant to act as a book of memories.

That was when the idea hit him.

He'd give Sara proof that he loved her. Straight from the

heart. And not with artificial headings created by someone else. It would be all in his own words.

The shop was closed, but he knew a place that stayed open late. A place where, with any luck, he'd find what he wanted.

To his relief, he found the perfect notebook. One with handmade pages, marbled edges and a teal suede cover. And, back in his flat, he sat at the table overlooking the Thames and began to write.

CHAPTER SIXTEEN

THE next morning at the crack of dawn, he walked up the stairs to Sara's flat. Rang the buzzer.

The intercom crackled. 'Yes?'

He recognised the voice instantly. 'Justin, it's Luke. I need to see Sara.'

'She doesn't need to see you.'

'Yes, she does.'

'If you hurt my sister you have me to deal with,' Justin warned.

Luke sighed. 'I'm not going to hurt Sara. I know I've screwed up—I'm here to fix it and make things right.' He took a gamble. 'I assume you know about the baby?'

'Yes.'

'And you know I asked her to marry me.'

'That's not quite how she sees it.'

'I screwed that up, too,' Luke admitted. 'There are a lot of things I need to say to her. A lot of things she needs to hear.'

'Only,' Justin said, 'if she wants to see you.'

'I'm not leaving until she sees me. If I have to, I'll camp on your doorstep,' Luke said.

'Ever heard of injunctions to stop stalkers?' Justin retorted.

'I'm not a stalker. I'm just an ordinary man who's made a mess of the most important thing that's ever happened to him. And I need a chance to put it right.'

'All right. Come up. But if she says no, you leave immediately,' Justin warned.

'Agreed. Thanks, Justin.'

Sara's brother didn't reply, but buzzed him up and met him outside the door. 'She's agreed to see you. So I'm giving you both space—but Sara has my number on speed dial.'

'She won't need it,' Luke promised.

'You look like hell,' Justin said, surprising him.

'I feel it,' Luke admitted. 'But it's no more than I deserve.'

He waited until Justin had left, then knocked on the door.

Sara opened it. She looked as bad as he felt; there were dark shadows under her eyes, her skin was pale and she looked as if she hadn't slept properly.

That made two of them. Except he'd been spared the morning sickness.

'Hi,' he said softly. 'Can I come in?'

She nodded and stepped aside.

'Thank you.' He dragged in a breath. 'I'm here to apologise—to tell you things I know I should've told you ages ago but…' He closed his eyes briefly. 'I don't find it easy to open up. But I know that's what it'll take to even start fixing things between us. And I'm prepared to do whatever it takes to make everything right again.'

'You'd better come through,' she said. 'Do you want something to drink?'

'No, thanks. Just to talk to you.' He followed her through to the living room; he wasn't surprised when she picked the chair, leaving him the sofa. He smiled wryly as he sat down. He had a long way to go. The only thing he could do was tell her the truth. Be honest. 'Nothing's seemed right since you left. Everything feels slightly out of shape, as if it doesn't fit. And it's made me realise that…' He dragged in a breath. 'I really hate having to admit this, but I need you.'

She said nothing, but he saw her eyes fill with tears.

'And I need to tell you something. About me. You once

asked me if I was part of a family business. Well, my family has a business. In the East End.'

She frowned. 'There's nothing wrong with the East End.'

'Most of it, I agree.' How could he explain? 'My family— they're what's known as…well, criminals.' Might as well tell her all of it. 'My dad's a thief, my grandad's a fraudster, my uncle's a fence. There's getaway drivers and muscle in the family, too. The kind of genes I didn't want to pass on.'

She went very still. 'So you're saying you want me to have a termination?'

'No. I said "didn't", not "don't". I'm trying to explain to you why I didn't want children. Remember I told you that my maths teacher spotted that I'd be good at economics?'

'Ye-es.'

'He told me at the police station—after I'd been arrested for shoplifting. He gave the police an assurance about me, and then started talking to me. He said I had a brain and, right then, I was wasting it. That if I carried on the way I was going, I'd end up so deep I'd never get out. That I could have a better life if I stayed on the right side of the law and used my natural talents.'

'So you took his advice?'

'I thought about it. Long and hard. And, yeah, I knew what he said made sense. It didn't go down well with the family, and it left me in a really awkward place. If I knew they were planning something and didn't try to stop them, that made me as bad as they were. An accomplice. But if I grassed them up to the police…'

'You were going against your own?' she guessed.

'Betraying my family.' He nodded. 'And that felt bad, too. For a while, I took the coward's way out and told them I'd keep quiet as long as I didn't know what they were doing.'

'The coward's way?'

'Because I should've shopped them.'

She frowned. 'Luke, how old were you when this happened?'

'Twelve.'

Her eyes widened. 'Luke, for pity's sake, you were still a child! There's nothing cowardly about what you did.'

'Hmm.' He wasn't so sure. 'Anyway. That teacher was the one who got me the market stall job and helped me keep straight. A few years later, I asked him why…and he said it was because he was like me once. Someone had helped him out, and he believed in…well, karma, I suppose. What goes around, comes around.'

'It does,' she said softly. 'So your family accepted it?'

He shook his head. 'It came to a head when I was fifteen. They wanted me to launder some money on the stall. I said no. It got messy. And in the end I gave them an ultimatum—accept that I wanted no part of what they did, or let me go.'

She bit her lip. 'And they let you go?'

'Even my mum turned her back on me.' It hurt to admit it.

'Your mum was a criminal, too?'

'No. She was…' He tried to think how best to explain. 'Fragile, I suppose. She found it easier to go with the flow. When Dad was inside, one of the family would come round and change fuses and fix leaks for her, that sort of thing. And they always made sure she was all right for money. I suppose they had a kind of honour—this thing about looking after your own.' He shrugged. 'The antidepressants took care of the rest of it. Dad would tell her what to say when the police came round, and she did it. So. That's why I don't—*didn't*—' he corrected himself swiftly '—do families.'

'I see.'

'And please don't get any rose-coloured-glasses ideas of getting me to make things up with them. I don't belong with them, and they don't belong with me. I don't want their kind of life—not for me, not for you and most definitely not for our baby.' He swallowed hard. 'But since I met you…I've learned something. I've realised that it doesn't matter where I came from. What matters is now. And I can make the family I want to be part of.' He looked at her. 'I want you, Sara. Being without you…it's like being back in those dark days, where I didn't believe in anything or anyone. When I kept everyone at a distance so they didn't have the chance to let me down.'

'I let you down, too,' she said. 'I walked out on you.'

'I pushed you into it. All I can say is that when you told me about the baby I panicked. And I swear I never meant to hurt you.'

'I saw all the walls go straight back up. And I didn't want to stay, drag you down until you resented me and the baby.'

'I'd never do that.'

'Wouldn't you?'

'No. Because I've learned the difference between what I thought I wanted, and what I really do want. I want a family, Sara. With you.'

'You offered me a business deal. A perfect contract,' she said. 'Not a family package.'

'And I was wrong. It isn't what I want, either.' There was nothing else for it. He was going to have to tell her. 'I won't blame you if you don't believe me, but I love you. And I can honestly say it's not just words for me. I've never said it to anyone else.'

And that was it. He'd given her all he had. Well, almost. He realised he was still clutching the paper carrier bag. He stood up and placed it in her lap. 'This isn't actually for you—it's for our baby, in years to come. But I'd like you to read it first.' He lifted a shoulder in a half-shrug. 'I'll see myself out. Call me if and when you want to talk.'

Sara didn't open the bag until after she'd heard the front door close behind him. She knew it had taken a lot for Luke to tell her the truth about his past. For a man who believed in straightforwardness and honour to admit that he'd grown up without either.

And the fact he'd said he loved her…

She believed that he hadn't said that to anyone else. That it had cost him a great deal to tell her. But could she let herself trust him? Could she believe that, if she went back to him, his barriers would stay down this time?

She opened the bag and took out the journal. Frowning, she opened the pages. It was hand-written, so he'd clearly taken the time to do this himself; he hadn't just dictated it for someone else to type up. So this was clearly important to him. Personal.

And he'd said it was for their baby.

She read on and realised he'd poured his heart out onto the pages. Telling their baby about her—what he loved about her, when he'd first realised that he loved her, how he felt when she was around. Admitting that part of him was scared to death that he wouldn't be a good enough father, but he was going to try because Sara had shown him what a family could be. How many things he was looking forward to—seeing their baby at the first scan, feeling the baby's first kicks, having that very first cuddle with a newborn. How he planned to spend time building sandcastles and paddling in the sea with their baby. Flying kites—the one good memory from his own childhood, one that he wanted to relive and share with their child—and having picnics at Greenwich. Being there to read a bedtime story; being there with a cuddle when their child woke in the night from a bad dream. And, most of all, being a family.

By the time she finished reading, Sara was bawling her eyes out. She rang Luke's mobile, but when he answered she was completely incoherent.

What seemed like seconds later, he was ringing the doorbell. She opened the door and just fell into his arms.

'I drove here as fast as I could. Are you all right? Is it the baby? Everything's going to be fine, honey. I'll call the ambulance. And I'm not going to leave you. Not now, not ever.'

He was halfway through punching in the emergency number when she stopped him. 'I don't need an ambulance,' she said shakily. 'The baby's fine.'

'Then why…?' He wiped her tears away gently with the pad of his thumb.

'I'm crying for you. For how much you missed out on as a child. But it's not going to be like that for our baby. We'll be a family—a real family. Because I love you, Luke. I really do love you.'

'Good. Because I love you all the way back. And it hurts like hell.'

'It doesn't have to any more.'

And then she was in his arms. Held so tightly that she could barely breathe—but she was holding Luke just as tightly. His mouth over hers, his kiss hot and demanding.

She'd untucked his shirt when he released her and took a step back.

'Luke?'

'I want you, Sara.' His voice had dropped an octave, and she could see the hunger in his eyes. 'But not here. It feels wrong.'

Disappointment clogged her throat. 'So what do you suggest?'

'Come home with me to the flat. *Our* flat,' he emphasised, 'for now. But if you want somewhere with a garden, we'll go house-hunting. Choose a place together.'

'But you love your flat. Your space.'

'It doesn't feel right without you. I need you, Sara.'

'And you'd really move, for me?'

'I'll do whatever it takes to make this right. To be a family with you. Because you and our baby are more important to me than anything else in the world.'

'Luke.' She kissed him hard.

It was less than twenty minutes before they were back at Luke's flat.

Less than one minute later before there was a trail of their clothes from the door to the bed.

And oh, it was good to feel his skin against hers, the warmth of his mouth as it teased hers to fever-pitch.

'Luke, you're driving me crazy. I need…'

'Me, too,' he said softly. 'But this time I want more. I want all the barriers gone. I want you and me, and nothing in between.'

'It's a bit late for contraception anyway,' she said shakily.

He kissed her and, as he eased into her, it felt like coming home. Making love with the man she loved more than anything—and who loved her all the way back.

She felt her body tightening round his, and his body surged in answer.

'Sara,' he whispered, 'I love you.'

'I love you, too.' And when she opened her eyes to look at him, she could see that his lashes were damp.

Afterwards she lay with her head on his shoulder, her hand resting on his chest and his fingers laced through hers.

'You're going to have to marry me, you know,' he said.

'Because of the baby?' That still stung.

'Because of *me*,' he corrected. 'I want to spend the rest of my days with you.'

'Luke, you're telling me. You're supposed to ask me properly.'

'I'm telling you because I don't want to risk you saying no.'

She smiled. 'What's that saying of yours? The one that annoys the hell out of me? Live a little.'

'You want me to ask you to marry me?'

'Give the monkey a peanut.'

'I love it when you're sassy with me.' He laughed. 'You'd better get dressed.'

'Why?'

'Because I'm not telling our children that I proposed to you stark naked.'

She couldn't help laughing back, but she did as he'd asked and got dressed. He pulled on his clothes and led her out to the bank of the Thames. Heedless of the people walking round them, he dropped down to one knee.

'Sara Fleet, I love you and you make my world a better place. I want to make a family with you. Will you marry me?'

There was a huge lump in her throat. But she managed to say the important word—the one she knew he was waiting for. 'Yes.'

From No. 1 *New York Times* bestselling author Nora Roberts

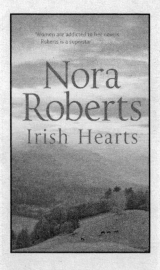

Two enthralling stories of Irish heroines with the courage to follow their dreams – and lose their hearts!

Containing the classic novels

Irish Thoroughbred

and

Irish Rose

Available 5th June 2009